*A Candlelight*
*Ecstasy Romance* ™

## HIS HYPNOTIC GAZE
## HELD HER MERCILESSLY. . . .

Leslie forced back the leaping flame of desire that was consuming her and made a half-hearted attempt at pulling her hand from his grasp. With one quick flick of his wrist, Cord jerked her down beside him.

She had only a moment before his mouth covered hers, and in that split second the strange glitter in his eyes was unreadable. All else was lost as the demanding insistence of his kiss began to force a response from her that was quickly turning into insatiable hunger. . . .

# LOVE HAS NO MERCY

*Eleanor Woods*

*A CANDLELIGHT ECSTASY ROMANCE* ™

Published by
Dell Publishing Co., Inc.
1 Dag Hammarskjold Plaza
New York, New York 10017

Dell ® TM 681510, Dell Publishing Co., Inc.

Candlelight Ecstasy Romance™ is a trademark of
Dell Publishing Co., Inc., New York, New York.

ISBN: 0-440-14611-9

Printed in the United States of America
First printing—October 1982

To Our Readers:

We have been delighted with your enthusiastic response to Candlelight Ecstasy Romances™ and we thank you for the interest you have shown in this exciting series.

In the upcoming months, we will continue to present the distinctive, sensuous love stories you have come to expect only from Ecstasy. We look forward to bringing you many more books from your favorite authors and also the very finest work from new authors of contemporary romantic fiction.

As always, we are striving to present the unique, absorbing love stories that you enjoy most—books that are more than ordinary romance.

Your suggestions and comments are always welcome. Please write to us at the address below.

Sincerely,

The Editors
Candlelight Romances

# LOVE HAS
# NO MERCY

# CHAPTER ONE

Leslie unfolded her considerable length from the confining space of the tiny red car, silently damning the designers who constructed such instruments of torture.

She ran a smoothing hand over her shoulder-length auburn hair and eyed the stocky figure of her co-worker as he removed himself from the "tomato can" with perfect ease.

"Why the frown, Les?" Jeremy asked, a cheeky grin on his pleasant face as he observed the angry glint in her green eyes.

"As if you didn't know," she replied sarcastically, flexing first one shoulder and then the other. "It's the last time, Jer, the very last time. I'll be damned if I'll be trussed up like a chicken and strapped in that—

that thing," she spluttered angrily. "From now on we'll take my car. At least I won't arrive at my destination with a crimp in my back."

Jeremy stared at her as if he were doubtful of her sanity. He ran a pudgy hand over the shiny surface of the fender nearest him, his face taking on the same expression of pride as a mother holding her first-born. "This little number is the ultimate in design, covering each phase of the problems facing us today," he expounded, reminding Leslie of an evangelist thumping away on the subject of hellfire and damnation. "There's fuel conservation: I average thirty-two miles per gallon on the road. Next there's the compactness. Someday we'll be squeezed off this planet by huge automobiles. Yessirree," he said with enthusiasm, "this is the car of the future."

Leslie could only stare at him disgustedly. "I'd rather ride a donkey. It would be infinitely more comfortable than that," she bluntly replied, waving one hand toward the object of her scorn.

"Has anyone ever told you that you're a snob, Leslie?" Jeremy questioned. He moved to the rear of the car and opened the trunk, muttering under his breath and wondering at the witlessness of all women.

"Now that you mention it, no." She leaned against the car in question and focused her attention on the rather sprawling house before her.

So this was the estate that Cord Langdon was giving to the organization that cared for young boys with behavorial problems. It was quite a gift, and one that was bound to endear him to the hearts of all concerned. But what lay behind such a generous offer?

Was he really that concerned for the youth of the city or was it simply an attempt to ingratiate himself with the local officials? But that was silly, he wasn't a resident of the area. The estate had been left to him by his aunt. Oh, well, she'd learn the answer as soon as she met the man.

To the right of the house Leslie caught a glimpse of the shimmering water of a swimming pool and a brightly striped umbrella in yellow and white. That would be an instant hit with the youngsters, as would the canal toward the rear of the property.

She couldn't help but feel sad at the thought of the old home becoming an institution. Hopefully the present structure would remain and not be torn down and replaced by a more modern building.

"I can see that you've fallen for that imposing pile of stone." Jeremy teased her with the casualness that comes with close friendship.

"Now that"—Leslie pointed at the house—"is worthy of one of your splendid speeches," she informed him, a warm smile curving her lips.

"No, thank you. I prefer a more modern dwelling. These old places leave me cold."

"Yes, one can tell." She glanced toward the car. "It's people like you who are slowly ridding this country of its history. If you're such a stickler for

11

modern structures, why did you do that series of photographs on Williamsburg? Surely you could have found some modern skyscraper that would have suited your needs just as well." It was an argument that went on continually between the two friends, aided by their almost mulish stubbornness.

"Do I have to fall in love with each subject in order to photograph it? Unlike you, I believe in progress."

"Progress has nothing to do with it. Can you imagine deserting that beautiful old place for some concrete monster in the city?" she asked derisively. "It's a disgrace."

"Well, don't go in there with fire in your eyes, for Pete's sake. Cord Langdon only agreed to this interview because of his long friendship with George."

"Oh, don't worry. I'm not so stupid as to jeopardize the assignment. But I've become somewhat suspicious of people who offer such generous gifts."

Jeremy rolled his eyes upward. "Why me, Lord? Of all the calm, unquestioning females, why should I be burdened with Joan of Arc?"

"Because, my aging Lothario, you can't abide their simpering ways. Besides, you know I need you," she added softly.

Jeremy fiddled with the strap of his camera and adjusted the light meter to his satisfaction. "Is it getting any easier?" he casually inquired.

"Yes. I've progressed to the point that it doesn't eat away at me anymore." But, she thought, how did one forget the little affairs that her husband had indulged in, and the first one only months after their wedding. The humiliation had been harsh and cruel. Leslie had fought for her marriage, but in their two years together, Charles had revealed a side of his personality that she was incapable of coping with.

A gentle touch on her arm brought her out of her unpleasant thoughts. "Let's go, Les. If we stand around here any longer, someone will think we're casing the joint." It was a silly remark leveled toward taking her mind off Charles Brien, and it worked.

One evening, about two months after leaving Charles and the city of Chicago behind and returning to Miami, Jeremy had brought the wine and Leslie had supplied the dinner. One drink led to another and, after far too many, she had given him an abbreviated version of her problems with Charles. Jeremy had listened with a straight face, but inwardly he'd been shocked. And yet he'd always suspected that Charles wasn't quite the polished individual he portrayed. Leslie's story merely confirmed his suspicions.

Leslie fingered the slim soft leather briefcase that was tucked under her arm as she walked beside Jeremy toward the imposing front entrance. She cast a quick glance at her friend and smothered a grin at the sight of his "stunning" profile, enhanced by the peculiar shape of his nose. On first meeting him, she had been unable to decide if that majestic protuberance had been an accident at birth, broken in a fight, or simply a genetic mix-up. Later she learned that his younger years as a promising boxer accounted for the misshapen appearance of that part of his face.

Jeremy gave the small black button a push and then stepped back. Leslie eyed the object with distaste. There should have been an impressive knocker on the heavy oak door. She slid one hand beneath the heavy curtain of her hair and lifted its thickness off her neck for a moment.

After waiting several seconds, Jeremy asked, "Are you sure about the time, Les?"

"Of course I'm sure," she snapped, pushing the collar of her blouse off her neck in the hope of catching a hint of the breeze coming off the canal. "I'm sorry, Jer, I shouldn't have snapped like that, but this heat is getting to me."

"Think nothing of it, honey. But are you sure it's the heat and not this interview?"

She leaned against the cool masonry, one long finger pressing with firm insistence on the doorbell. "Oh, it's not the interview, that'll be a breeze. It's just that George was so emphatic that I do it. I had to juggle my schedule and wound up with Miriam taking two of my appointments. I've never seen him act like that before. He waved aside my protests as if they didn't matter at all."

"I agree that it doesn't sound like our boss. Perhaps he was worried that another magazine would get the story," Jeremy reasoned. "Were you able to research our man of mystery?"

Leslie shrugged. "I spent most of the morning on it. Mr. Langdon is quite popular with the ladies. There's a number of photographs showing him with various women. He's also very wealthy. I wonder how he and George became such good friends. George is certainly not the playboy type."

"Who knows? George did say that the interview was to cover only the very generous gift of the estate and not in any way cover Mr. Langdon's personal life. Did you get the same instructions?"

"The very same. He seems to have an aversion to reporters. I wonder why." She looked at the slim gold watch on her wrist and then at Jeremy. "Do you suppose he really might have second thoughts about seeing us?"

"He could have, but I doubt it. More likely he's been held up or he's outside and didn't hear the bell. You wait here while I take a look around and shoot some background. At least we'll have accomplished something."

"Thanks, Jer. Let's hang around another ten minutes or so, and if he hasn't shown up, we'll go. George can hardly find fault with that," she reasoned with a shrug.

After Jeremy disappeared around the corner of the house, Leslie looked about resignedly. The only decent seat were the chairs by the tables around the pool. Since she was somewhat reluctant to take such liberties, there was nothing to do but join the search or lounge as gracefully as possible on the top step.

After another go with the doorbell she did just that. In her mind it was another mark against the sybaritic life led by the idle rich. It was inordinately rude to keep a person waiting. Her thoughts became lost in painful reflection of the number of times Charles had deliberately held up their arrival at a party or some other event in order to make an entrance.

Her unpleasant reverie was broken by the sound of the large front door opening. Leslie came to her feet in a graceful move, straightening the pale yellow silk blouse and smoothing the material of the light beige skirt over her slim hips.

She was aware of being observed and raised her eyes to meet the sardonic gaze of the tall figure standing in the now opened door. She lifted her chin, calmly returning the openly appraising examination. There was a sinister look about the man that caused a shiver of fear to race along her spine. The craggy features of his face were harsh and unyielding, the indomitable thrust of chin and jaw an indication of suppressed violence. His dark eyes were fringed with thick lashes as black as his brows which were drawn together in a speculative fashion.

For a moment Leslie was faced with the ridiculous notion that if a match was struck too close to him, he would explode. Never had she encountered anyone so vitally alive. He exuded sex appeal and a distinct maleness that even Leslie was forced to admit was unusual.

He stepped forward, his head towering over hers as he halted just in front of her. "Miss Garrison?" he asked pleasantly, something flickering in the depths of his dark eyes. It was difficult to form an impression, but Leslie was certain there had been a slight start when he'd first seen her.

"Yes, I'm Leslie Garrison." She held out a slim hand, finding it remarkably refreshing to have to look up at him. Being five feet seven inches in her stocking feet reduced, rather dramatically, the number of men for a woman of her height. "You are Cord Langdon, aren't you?" she asked in a friendly voice.

"That's correct," he answered, inclining his head in assent, the clasp of his hand warm and strong. "I'm sorry you were kept waiting. I was in the shower, and my housekeeper is out. Please, come this way." He indicated the walk that led to the pool. Leslie cast a regretful look toward the house and then followed him.

He was dressed casually in denims and a short-sleeved pullover, the darkness of his clothing setting off his deep tan. As she walked behind him, Leslie's eyes quickly took in the thick black hair, the powerfully built shoulders, and the broad chest. His body was devoid of fat, the muscle tone in perfect harmony with his lean tall length.

When they came to a step in the walk, he turned and offered his hand. Leslie hesitated only momentairly before touching him again, but the rapier-sharp gaze missed nothing. "Have you forgotten your camera?" he casually inquired after they were over the rough spot. He led her over to a white table and pulled out a chair.

"I won't be taking the photographs. Jeremy Keyes will be doing those," she informed him. She took the offered seat and then arranged her features to reflect a pleasant but professional interest only. "He's the photographer; I'll be handling the interview." She waited a moment. "Is that agreeable with you?"

He made a deprecatory gesture with one hand. "Of course. George didn't tell me about him, so I naturally assumed you would be doing both jobs."

"Well, he's about, I assure you. He's getting some outside shots of the house and grounds at the moment." She wished to emphasize Jeremy's presence.

Her host leaned back in the fragile wrought iron chair in a perfectly relaxed pose. "Tell me, Miss Garrison, how long have you been with George? I've been in and out of his place a number of times and I don't remember seeing you." His question was put in a friendly manner, but Leslie had the distinct feeling he was mentally compiling a dossier on her.

"I've known Mr. Corstairs for a number of years. He's a friend of my dad's and gave me my first job. He very kindly set about educating me in some of the more practical aspects of journalism." She smiled. "Like most graduates in any chosen field, I was ready to set the world on fire with my knowledge. Mr. Corstairs, without completely destroying my self-es-

18

teem, took me in hand and attempted to make a journalist of me."

"Was he successful?" he asked.

"Yes." She answered unhesitatingly. "I think I'm quite good at my job."

"And?" he prodded, as he removed the wrapper from a slim cigar. The click of his lighter sounded loud in the quiet stillness of their surroundings.

"And?" she repeated, knowing full well what he was hinting at, but parrying the question skillfully.

"How long have you been with him? Do you like your job? Tell me something about yourself." His bold gaze noted the flush that stole over the delicate curve of her cheeks.

Leslie gave him a feigned look of surprise and said, "I'm sorry, Mr. Langdon, but apparently there's been some mistake. I assumed Mr. Corstairs had cleared it with you for me to conduct this interview." Her gaze never wavered. "If there's some question regarding my qualifications, I'll be only too happy to wait while you telephone my office. Otherwise I'd like to get started."

He observed her for a moment, a spark of admiration entering his dark eyes. "Touché, Miss Garrison." He smiled. "I'm sure you're a credit to your profession. Please, let's get on with it."

For the next thirty minutes or so things went smoothly. He was cooperative to a fault, answering each of her questions with complete candor. From past experience Leslie was vitally aware of the importance of a person's willingness in relation to the success of the article.

"Would I be correct, Mr. Langdon, in assuming that your generous gift is simply the fulfillment of your aunt's dream?"

The dark head nodded in agreement. "You could assume that." For some reason Leslie felt a sense of hostility emanating from him as she pursued the subject of his aunt.

"Was it a specific request in her will or had the two of you discussed the dispensation of the estate prior to her death?" she persisted, still not satisfied with his indifference.

"Miss Garrison, my aunt left the entire estate to me. As I'm sure you're aware, I have no need for the place. I made the decision to turn it over to the Leher Foundation. I'm afraid I really can't tell you if my Aunt Agatha would have approved or not. But I'm sure the youngsters will." He looked out over the wide sweep of lawn, a grim look on his face. "I think it fitting that young people enjoy this place."

Leslie's hand flew across the pages of her pad as she took down his words. It was frustrating to be hindered by a direct order from George. He'd said no questions regarding Cord Langdon's personal life, but Leslie knew there was a story beneath the hint of bitterness in his voice. The man seated opposite her felt no love for his aunt. The estate was unimportant to him, merely an encumbrance, another responsibility.

She itched to question him further, but orders were orders. Besides, George had acted so peculiar about the assignment Leslie was hesitant about going against his wishes. Even being as good friends as they were, she would never deliberately disregard a direct order. But there were other ways of learning the truth. It would simply require more time than she'd anticipated.

"May I ask you a question, Miss Garrison?"

"Of course," she automatically replied without looking up from her notes, her mind busy forming her next round of questions.

"Are you engaged?" His eyes studied her left hand and the ring that had belonged to her mother. It was old-fashioned in design, unusual and attractive, the delicate filigree surrounding the three diamonds.

"No," she quickly shot back, not in the least put off, at least outwardly, by the sudden change of pace. *Very smart, Mr. Langdon, very smart,* she thought to herself. She wondered if he'd sensed she was becoming more than a little curious and was attempting to throw her off the track.

"Is it an unmentionable?" he persisted. A muscle twitched at one corner of his mouth as he witnessed the tight control she was exercising over her temper.

"Not at all." She looked up from her notes, meeting his bold gaze without the slightest hesitation. "Now, may we get on with the interview?" she asked in a businesslike manner.

Cord leaned forward, his tanned forearms resting

on the table. Leslie couldn't help but notice the fine hairs on his arms, bleached a lighter shade by the sun. He was a very attractive man, and under other circumstances she might have responded to his slight overture. But somehow his assured manner and authoritative gestures reminded her of another man that had seemed so perfect.

"Is there any law that says we have to finish this chore today?" There was a hint of mischief lurking in his eyes that annoyed her. "I'm sure George isn't that much of a tyrant."

"Chore, Mr. Langdon?" she asked in mock surprise, a pert smile touching the curve of her generous mouth. "You've really pricked my ego. Here I've been congratulating myself on a job well done and all the while you've been bored. My, my," she murmured in a somber tone. "Another ten minutes and we would have been finished."

Cord observed her little performance with one dark brow arched in wry amusement. "Oh, believe me, Miss Garrison, you've done an excellent job," he replied knowingly. "I must remember to congratulate George on the exceptional capabilities of his staff." He sighed deeply, a resigned look on his face. "Another ten minutes did you say?"

"Scout's honor," she answered brightly. The skirmish had been short and lively, but Leslie had enjoyed the brief exchange and the fact that she felt she was winning.

She kept a close check on her watch, and even

though she longed to throw caution to the wind, she suppressed the impulse. After the final question had been asked and answered, Leslie placed her pad and pencil in her briefcase and smiled. "You've been very patient, Mr. Langdon. Thank you." A quick thrust of her legs against the chair allowed her enough room to stand.

Cord too had risen and was regarding her with open admiration. "My pleasure, Miss Garrison." His deep voice was soft and gentle.

A sudden gust of wind from the canal blew across the pool, causing the ends of Leslie's hair to flutter across her face. Before she could remove the clinging strands, Cord reached across the width of the table and gently caught the silken tendrils and tucked them behind her ear.

It was only after he removed his hand that Leslie realized she had been holding her breath. The touch of his hand on the side of her face had been soft, almost sensuous in its gentleness.

Neither of them were aware of Jeremy, who was standing regarding them, his light blue eyes narrowed in speculation. "I see that you found Mr. Langdon, Leslie." He spoke casually, aware of the air of electricity surrounding the two.

## CHAPTER TWO

"Yes," she answered, more grateful than she realized for the interruption. "You were gone so long, I'd begun to wonder," she casually remarked, clamping a tight rein on her emotions.

He shrugged his shoulders, an apologetic grin on his face. "Sorry, but I sort of lost track of time. There really should be some great shots though."

The introductions were made, and then Cord surprised Leslie by inviting them in for a drink. Jeremy was quick to accept, but Leslie declined as gracefully as she could.

"But I understood the house was of paramount importance to this interview, Miss Garrison," her host said. "When I talked with George, he indicated the desire for a full spread of photographs of the interior as well as the grounds." The stubborn thrust of his jaw added to the determination that was hinted at in the silken tones of his deep voice.

Leslie glanced at Jeremy, but from the blandly innocent look she received in return, it was evident no help would be forthcoming from that quarter. "Perhaps another time, Mr. Langdon. Jeremy is capable of handling his end of the assignment without my interference."

"Nonsense, Les. A woman's touch would be welcome in this particular job," Jeremy reasoned with a perfectly straight face. "Besides, it would save me another trip."

*Damn you,* Leslie silently fumed. She wanted to get away from Cord Langdon! He saw too much with those mysterious dark eyes, presenting her with a challenge each time she met them. And if there was one thing Jeremy didn't need, it was her help. His ability to capture that elusive "something" so important in a truly great photograph was widely known.

Cord choose that moment to intervene. "Only ten minutes, Miss Garrison?" The quick play on words brought an involuntary smile to her lips in spite of the tiny voice urging her to be careful.

"Scout's honor, Mr. Langdon?"

"Scout's honor, Miss Garrison."

"Then I'd be happy to accept." After all, winning one battle from such a worthy opponent was enough for one day. She could afford to be generous.

Cord opened the door and ushered them inside.

The foyer was spacious, the floor done in an intricate mosaic pattern, worn in places from years of traffic. There were matching oval openings on each side that led to what appeared to be a large living room on the right—to the left was a library-cum-office.

He moved toward the living room and indicated that they should precede him. It was bright and airy due to the French doors leading onto a large patio and one wall given over to floor-to-ceiling windows.

Leslie's attention was immediately drawn to a grouping of watercolors hanging on one wall. The composition, while somewhat amateurish, was nevertheless rather appealing.

"My aunt enjoyed dabbling in oils and watercolors. You'll find a number of her paintings scattered throughout the house," Cord informed her.

The furniture was a mixture of old and modern. There were worn leather pieces arranged without apology among the antiques. Every available surface as well as several glass-front cabinets held the strangest assortment of things Leslie had ever seen. Some were quite beautiful; others were hideous.

"Rather a remarkable collection, wouldn't you say?" Cord remarked with a wry twist of his mouth. "I'm afraid she wasn't very discriminating when it came to collecting." He walked over to a low cabinet and opened the double doors to reveal several bottles of liquor. "What would you like to drink, Miss Garrison, Mr. Keyes?"

"Scotch and water will do nicely," replied Jeremy,

his face alight with interest as he walked around the room. "May I wander for a few minutes?" he inquired of their host as he accepted his drink.

"Of course, be my guest. Miss Garrison and I will wait for you here." After Jeremy had gone, Cord turned to Leslie. "You haven't told me what you would like to drink," he reminded her softly.

Leslie forced herself to meet and hold his gaze. *No, Leslie,* the tiny voice cautioned, *don't even think of it. Once burned . . . remember?* "Something cool, please." Her voice was unconsciously husky. The brief moment of victory, due to the completion of the interview and the gentle sparring they had enjoyed, slowly faded, replaced by a feeling of emptiness. It would be unbelievably stupid to allow herself even to think of becoming involved with Cord Langdon.

While they waited for Jeremy to finish, both Cord and Leslie were careful to choose topics of conversation that were about as appealing as dust. The same tenseness that had been present by the pool seemed to pervade the room.

After Jeremy had finished and he and Leslie were leaving, Cord shook hands with the photographer and assured him that he was welcome anytime to take additional pictures. He turned to Leslie, his enigmatic gaze sweeping her from head to toe. "And if there's any further information needed for the article, Miss Garrison, please let me know. This has been a most pleasurable experience. And you're right— you are good at your job."

Leslie thanked him and quickly followed Jeremy to the car. She resisted the almost overwhelming urge to turn and look back. Had she done so, she would have been perplexed by the pleased expression on Cord's rugged face. Her puzzlement would have taken on even greater proportions had she been privy to his telephone conversation with George upon reentering the house. Even George was taken aback when Cord asked if the offer of an office was still open. Upon the swift assurance that it was, the two men went on to discuss exactly what would be needed in way of furnishings.

During the ride back to the office, Jeremy made several attempts at conversation. If he noticed Leslie's less than enthusiastic participation, he didn't comment, for which she was grateful. She'd met a number of men since her divorce, but Cord Langdon didn't seem to fit into any of the carefully labeled slots she'd so painstakingly constructed. Meeting him had left her with a feeling of discontent that was annoying.

"I think you were a hit with our Mr. Langdon," Jeremy casually remarked, causing Leslie to snap out of her reflective mood with a start.

She shot a quick look at him. "What makes you say that?"

"Well"—he ran one hand round the back of his neck and then cocked his head slightly—"it's not likely that he'd have gone out of his way to be so accommodating, even if he is a friend of George's.

And the looks he was giving you were something else." At her indifferent shrug he said, "Don't give me that I'm-not-interested look, Les. The two of you were involved in some sort of mental struggle the moment you met."

Leslie merely gave him a chilling look and sighed. Regardless of what she said, it wouldn't change Jeremy's mind. She didn't breathe easily until they turned into the underground parking garage of the tall impersonal building that housed *Preview*.

Jeremy brought the car to a halt in the parking space assigned him and turned to face Leslie. "Still miffed with me?" He grinned.

She was tempted to answer with a stinging retort, but he was too good a friend. "No." She shook her head. "But please keep your ridiculous opinions to yourself. I'd be the laughing-stock of the office if they got out." She opened the door and stepped out. "See you tomorrow." With a wave of her hand she walked toward her car.

She had no plans for the evening and it would be an excellent time to work on her notes to prepare for her meeting with George the next day. It would also give her an excellent opportunity to tackle him about the rather peculiar circumstances surrounding the interview. There was a story there, and she wanted it.

By the time she'd struggled through the five o'clock traffic and reached her apartment, Leslie was steaming from the heat. She entered the cool living room and gave a sigh of pure pleasure. After thumbing through the mail, she tossed her handbag and the letters on the sofa and strode purposefully toward the bedroom.

She stripped off the sticky clothes and in minutes she was standing beneath the shower. While she gave in to the physical pleasure of the water cooling her heated body, her mind was still attempting to come to grips with the disturbing picture of a deeply tanned face with dark eyes watching her with an intentness that was very disconcerting.

As she soaped one shapely leg, she shook her head in an irritated gesture. Any woman silly enough to become involved with Cord Langdon was asking for trouble. According to his file he was thirty-six and had never been married. If he hadn't met someone by this time, it was fairly obvious he wasn't interested in any sort of relationship other than that of the typical playboy flitting from one brief affair to the next.

Leslie stepped out of the shower and rubbed her body dry with a soft fluffy towel before liberally applying her favorite dusting powder. Just as she reached to open the door, the telephone started ringing. She grabbed the white terry robe and shrugged into it as she hurried to answer.

"Hello," she said rather breathlessly. The receiver was cradled between her cheek and shoulder, leaving her hands free to fasten the robe.

"Leslie? How are you?" an excited voice cried.

"Siri? Good Lord, you sound so close. Are you in Miami?" Her mind immediately took stock of the available food and wine. Also the complete havoc that seemed to surround her petite friend. Leslie sat on the side of the bed in preparation for the long conversation to come.

"No, no, I'm afraid it'll be some time before I can get away. I was just thinking of you and decided to call. How are you? Your letters have begun to taper off, so what gives?"

Leslie laughed at the demanding tone. "I'm sorry, Siri, but I'm completely swamped with work. I'll try to do better, I promise. But enough about me, how are you?"

"Great. Pete and I are still seeing each other, and the gallery is coming along nicely. I'm hoping this will be my best year."

They talked on with Siri bringing Leslie up-to-date on all the gossip of who was seeing whom and so on. "By the way, have you heard from Charles?" she asked.

"Charles? Heavens, no. I haven't seen him since the party at Vivian's. Why?" Leslie quickly asked.

"Well, I thought I'd better warn you," her friend replied drily. "I ran into him at dinner last night and he was making noises about going to Miami and making you listen to reason. Of course, he was slightly drunk, so it might be just talk. But with Charles one never knows."

Leslie chewed at her bottom lip as she absorbed

this latest bit of information regarding her ex-husband. It had been almost a year since their divorce. Surely he wasn't considering a reconciliation. "Thanks, Siri, I'll be prepared. But the last I heard, Susie Crain was almost certain to be the next Mrs. Brien."

"I think it was more her idea than his. He's taken the divorce hard, Les. So if he does come down there, for goodness' sake don't feel sorry for him and do something foolish. I told him quite a few home-truths about himself when he told me of his plans. I'd been itching to do it for ages."

Leslie chuckled. Even Charles was to be pitied. Siri possessed a wealth of love for her friends, the finesse of a steamroller, and the memory of an elephant. To her way of thinking Charles had treated Leslie abominably. It didn't require much imagination to visualize the pint-sized brunette giving him the tongue-lashing of his life.

"I'm sure you rose to the occasion beautifully, Siri, and thanks. But don't worry about me taking him back. I've served my period of indenture—let someone else have the pleasure." Another fifteen minutes went by before the connection was broken. Leslie replaced the receiver, smiling as she shook her head in disbelief. Dealing with Siri often taxed one's mental processes to the limit.

She reached beneath the spread for the pillows and then stacked them against the headboard. She leaned back, Siri's conversation opening the door to her past with cold certainty. She remembered the last time she'd seen Charles. It had been at a party given by the Krones. They hadn't been particularly good friends of Leslie's, but it was one of those invitations that she felt she should accept.

The divorce from Charles had only been granted three days before the party. Leslie was well aware of Vivian's reputation as a gossip but decided to accept the invitation anyway.

"I'm so sorry, Leslie, but I had no idea Ted had invited Charles and Susie," her hostess had said gushingly as she took Leslie's wrap, her squinty eyes alert to the tiniest indication of embarrassment.

*I just bet you didn't,* Leslie longed to shout. Instead, she gave her a bright smile, effectively suppressing the feeling of rage that surged throughout her body. "Nonsense, darling, Charles and I are adults, so don't give it another thought." As Leslie turned to speak to someone else she'd been amused by the expression of puzzlement in Vivian's eyes.

Charles had retained enough decency to be profoundly embarrassed at seeing her. A dark flush had slowly risen from his neck to cover his face when he turned to find Leslie laughing and talking with a small group. Their glances locked, and Leslie had shown no mercy in the contemptuous thrust of her chin as she regarded him.

Susie had reacted like a frightened mouse, her Barbie-doll paleness pathetically lacking in comparison to Leslie's tall, slim beauty.

The only bright spot of the evening had been Vivian's disappointment. Leslie had been unable to resist a typical bitchy jab as she was leaving. "I'm so sorry, darling, that your evening didn't go as planned, but then, you can never tell about people, can you?" She laughed all the way to the waiting cab.

Thinking of that little tidbit of perfect feminine revenge did much to lighten Leslie's mood for the remainder of the evening. And after a sandwich and a glass of milk, she sorted her notes and began typing a rough draft of her interview with Cord Langdon.

The next morning Leslie entered her small office with a sense of satisfaction. After removing the cover from her typewriter and readying her desk for the busy day ahead, she reached for her briefcase and removed the typewritten pages that she had completed the evening before.

She studied the article critically, and while it wasn't a subject to interest people of all ages, it warmly reflected the generosity of Cord Langdon and touched on the realization of a dream come true for the Leher Foundation.

She was still reading, toying with a pencil with one hand, a frown marring her forehead, when Miriam Ely came through. She stopped and walked back to look pointedly at her young assistant. "Heavens! From the unpleasant look on your face, I would definitely stop reading whatever it is you're laboring over." She moved around and peered over Leslie's shoulder so that she could see what was causing such anxiety. After a few minutes of quick scanning she said, "Not bad."

Leslie swung her chair around and smiled cheekily. "I agree, it serves its purpose. But"—she fixed her boss with a questioning look—"have you ever had the feeling that something's missing?" She pointed to the pages in her left hand. "Not with the article, I'm pleased with that. It's the man that puzzles me."

Miriam gave her one of her approving nods and then perched on the edge of the desk. "Explain, please. I've met Cord several times, but I've never considered him puzzling. Frankly, I find him to be a very sexy character."

"Actually, I wasn't thinking of him in terms of his sex appeal—that goes without saying. It's his relationship with his aunt that's the mystery. I definitely detected a sense of anger . . . bitterness . . . in his voice when he spoke of her. I wonder why?"

Miriam gave an indifferent shrug. "I've no idea. Is it important to the article?"

"No," Leslie replied, "but it's there, and I'm naturally curious. But I didn't dare delve deeper because of George," she explained.

"How did Cord strike you as a person?"

Leslie was slow in answering. "Dynamic. Incredibly sexy. As you say, he's one of the most attractive men I've ever met. But not in the conventional sense. He's not what I'd call handsome."

"But he leaves you cold," Miriam stated knowingly.

"No," Leslie readily admitted. "But on the other hand, I'm not so foolish as to want to become involved with him. At the moment I prefer someone less volatile." She regarded Miriam thoughtfully. "Is this another attempt to get me into the swing of things as you and George believe I should be?" A resigned expression covered her face.

"Well," the older woman hedged, "he is a close friend of George's, and we thought it would be a nice way for you to meet him. He's entirely different from the men you've been going out with. Most of them resemble the tame inhabitants of a children's zoo."

"Miriam, when will you get it through your head that I prefer that sort of man at the moment. Cord Langdon reminds me too much of Charles."

"You've got to be kidding! How can you possibly compare the two?" she spluttered.

"Perhaps not physically, but basically I think they're the same. I have no desire to become one in a long line of has-beens. A casual affair with your hero is not what I want at the moment," she stated firmly. "And just out of curiosity, how did you and George plan to pull off your little coup? Did it ever occur to either of you that he might not care for me?"

"Honestly, Leslie, we weren't planning on holding a gun to your heads. George simply thought the two of you might click. But if you didn't, well, that's that." She smiled. "If I were fifteen, even ten years younger, we wouldn't be having this ridiculous con-

36

versation. I'd catch that man so quickly he'd be weeks wondering what had happened."

"Heavens, Miriam, I never knew a mere man could arouse you so," Leslie teased.

"I'm in the later summer of my years, Leslie, not the frozen winter." She came to her feet in a decisive move. "Don't forget, you're to cover the opening of the new art museum this evening."

"I'll remember."

Leslie turned back to her desk, somewhat touched by the kindly efforts of George and Miriam. For however interfering and ridiculous some of their shenanigans were, they cared.

Miriam's expression of disbelief when Leslie had stated her lack of interest in Cord Langdon was comical. But past mistakes have a way of making a person cautious. And while she quite possibly would enjoy going out with Cord Langdon, she wasn't the sort to pine away with disappointment. She was popular and never without a date, if she chose to accept.

After her impromptu meeting with Miriam, and in the course of the morning, Leslie was kept busy. It was as though everyone was having some sort of party or get-together and simply must have Leslie in attendance. The events ranged from a very top-drawer society wedding to a young and promising designer's showing of her new fall fashions.

Some of the requests were from friends and were newsworthy and she would attend. The others Leslie

37

put off with "It's such short notice, dear, but I'll try." It was impossible to be everyplace at once, but that was part of the challenge of her job. It was interesting and fast-paced, and it suited her.

Occasionally she was struck with the frightening thought that if she weren't careful she could quite easily become another Miriam. And while she admired the older woman, it wasn't in her scope of things to grow old alone.

Lunch was spent with Carol Eddy, George's receptionist. The two women had been friends for years and made a point to lunch together when their schedules permitted.

Carol sank into the chair and gave a deep sigh. Leslie sent her a knowing smile and asked, "Have George and Miss Langley been especially testy this morning?"

"Testy hardly covers it." She rolled her eyes upward in dismay. "Honestly, Les. Miss Langley should have been a warden. She literally stalks that poor young girl that works under her. I couldn't stand it."

Leslie laughed helplessly at the picture she painted of her tormentor. First impressions were of a sweet, fragile little lady in her early fifties. Closer inspection revealed an iron will, equal to the great Indian chief, Cochise. She was like a dragon in her protection of George, shielding him from anything that might cause him the slightest worry. She'd been known to reduce angry men, rude society matrons, and less important underlings to a state of stammering indecision in a matter of seconds. No one, regardless of rank or status, was excused if they threatened George's peace of mind.

"What or who has had the effrontery to ruffle her feathers this time?" inquired Leslie.

"Some to-do about Cord Langdon. He's here, as you know, you lucky dog, to dispose of the estate left him by his aunt. Since they're such close friends, George had an office placed at his disposal. Of course, this required extra work for the dragon lady."

At that moment their waitress appeared to take their orders. After making their choice, the conversation resumed.

"Don't worry about Cord Langdon. He'll have Miss Langley eating out of his hand in no time at all. He can be extremely charming," Leslie informed Carol in a dry voice. She wondered why he was taking an office. Miriam hadn't mentioned it earlier.

They talked on, touching on various subjects. Even the arrival of their food slowed the flow of conversation only slightly.

"By the way," remarked Leslie, "Siri called last night. We talked for almost an hour. She sends you regards and hopes to see us sometime in the future. Which, knowing her as I do, could mean anything from next week to next year," she laughingly explained.

"Well, whenever, it should be an exciting time

ahead," grinned Carol. "Things have a way of becoming incredibly mixed up when she's around." Carol had met Siri when she'd visited Leslie in Chicago, so an explanation of her "unusual" personality wasn't needed. She threw a quick glance at Leslie and then asked, "I assume Charles is alive and kicking?"

"Of course. That's one reason for the call. He hinted that he was thinking of paying me a visit. Of course, Siri almost had a spasm."

"I can imagine. She would never forgive you if you weakened and took him back. As a matter of fact, neither would I," Carol bluntly declared.

"Go back to Charles? My God! Perish the thought. As for forgiving me, you'd have to get in line to heap recriminations down on my head." She took a sip of coffee. "I never dreamed he was disliked by so many of my friends. Later, yes. But even my dad confessed to being less than pleased with our marriage."

"Would you have listened had he offered an opinion before the nuptials?" Carol asked with a wry grin.

Leslie shook her head. "No. Unfortunately, I'm so headstrong, I have to learn the hard way."

After she was back at her desk, Leslie considered the nagging piece of information Carol had passed on. Knowing Cord had an office in the same building was something to think about.

She'd denied, rather strongly, to Miriam that she

was interested in him, even allowed Carol to think she was indifferent. But deep down she knew the opposite to be true. She *was* interested in him, and it was a damned nusiance!

# CHAPTER THREE

From the moment their eyes met and held, Leslie had been intensely aware of Cord. It was funny how she had even begun to think of him by his first name. But the bit about him reminding her of Charles was true. For he too had been charming, sweeping away a young and impressionable Leslie along with the tide of infatuation that overwhelmed her.

As she worked at her desk, Leslie was suddenly stricken with an embarrassing thought. Had George the audacity to inform Cord of his idiotic notion of playing cupid? Did that account for his attempt to get her to ditch the interview? Had he merely been testing her?

She hurried across the room to the door of Miriam's office. "Do you have a minute?" she asked.

Miriam looked up from the work she was going over. Her narrow reading glasses were perched on the end of her nose, lending a comical air to an otherwise attractive face. "Of course, dear. What can I help you with?" She indicated the soft leather armchair situated at the corner of her desk.

Leslie sat down, a mutinous look on her face. "Did George by any chance make Cord Langdon aware of his little game of matchmaking?"

Miriam laughed at the stern look on Leslie's face. "Are you asking if you were set up? No. I was going to do the interview, but one word led to another and," she confessed, "I suppose you could say I'm the culprit. George was explaining about Cord, his success, how he was giving the estate to charity, and so on. It struck me that you might like to meet him."

"Then why was George so adamant against an in-depth interview?"

Miriam smiled. "That part is legitimate. Cord's been linked with any number of women. His name has even been mentioned in a couple of divorces, erroneously so by the press, so he isn't that fond of any sort of reporters. He has a natural aversion to the press."

"So it wasn't something trumped up just to throw us together?" she continued stubbornly.

"Not at all. George had spoken with him months ago when he first learned of the gift." She reached for the case that held her cigarettes and removed one and lit it. "Don't feel angry at us, Leslie."

"Oh," she shook her head, "I'm not, although I am relieved. Honestly, Miriam, more time has been spent on trying to correct my unmarried state than is applied to the national debt. I've met cousins, brothers—'He's such a nice man, Leslie,'—I know immediately that I can count on a shy, homely introvert or a macho wonder intent on satisfying the deprived state of my libido."

"Leslie!" cried Miriam, as she sat back in her chair and laughed helplessly.

"I'm not kidding. I've become paranoid on the subject of suitable escorts," she ruefully admitted.

Later, back at her desk, Leslie was annoyed to find her thoughts turning more and more to Cord's sudden appearance in her life. At one point she was shocked by her mental exercise as she wondered what it would be like to be kissed by him. *You poor thing,* she sighed disgustedly, *you've got Cord Langdon on the brain.*

During the course of the afternoon Jeremy stopped by to show her the layout of prints he'd taken that would accompany her article on Cord.

Leslie went through them, more than ever impressed by Jeremy's fantastic ability to speak with pictures. "You've outdone yourself, as usual." She handed them back, a pleased smile on her face. "I think the end result will be very satisfying for us both."

"Thanks. By the way, Jim can't make it this evening, so I'll be going with you to the museum opening," he informed her in a resigned tone.

Leslie grinned at his aggrieved manner. "Now, now," she teased. "Let's not be nasty. I know it's not your favorite sort of gathering, but it is of social importance. Without those little affairs I'd be stuck behind a desk all day, and you might be a plumber."

"A plumber? Thanks, Leslie, you have the innate ability to make one feel so needed . . . so useful." He scowled, giving her a mean look.

"Simply keeping you in line, Jer. You do tend to look down on us lesser mortals. I enjoy watching you turn red in the face."

"I'll get you back, just you wait. I'll arrange for 'Miss Prunes' to give you a guided tour of the place this evening," he taunted. Leslie heartily disliked the lady in question. But worst of all, Leslie knew Jeremy would do it. The pranks they pulled on each other were wild and numerous.

Her green eyes fairly glowed as she digested his latest threat, and her own reply was equally as mean. "If you sic that irritating old bitch on me, I'll spread some wild tale about you that will completely ruin you with that cute little blonde in the typing pool."

"What a horrifying thought," he grinned. "You win, but you'd better watch your step," he threatened as he left her office.

Later, as she was clearing her desk before leaving for the day, Miriam walked through. "Would you really do such a thing, Leslie?" she asked, a twinkle in her eyes.

Leslie looked at her for a moment, her mind completely blank. "Do what?"

"Spread some wild story about Jeremy?"

"No, but he's not sure," she grinned impishly. "On the other hand, I'm not sure either. After him running my name through that computer-dating thing, and that weird little man that showed up at my apartment, I just might."

Miriam only shook her head and laughed. "The two of you are nuts." With a wave of her hand she left.

Leslie quickly finished up and followed suit. If she was lucky, she'd have time enough for a nice long soak in a warm tub before Jeremy picked her up. With none other than this pleasant thought in mind, she left her office, closing the door behind her. She walked down the hall toward the elevator, her long, tan legs in the attractive high-heeled sandals covering the distance with ease. She pressed the button and then stepped back and waited.

Her body unconsciously struck an attractive pose, her auburn hair and the light golden tan of her complexion an unusual but attractive combination. She'd long ago accepted the fact that God had been more than generous in dispensing good looks her way. She'd never dwelled on the matter, merely accepting it as an ordinary happening.

She was watching the numbers light up the panel

of the indicator, when the elevator stopped and opened. The fast forward motion of her body brought her up against the solid wall of a hard chest. Two strong arms closed about her in a tight embrace. "My, my, such enthusiasm," the teasing voice spoke.

Leslie's gaze traveled upward along the strong column of a tanned neck, past the sensuous curve of a smiling mouth until her green eyes encountered a pair of dark brown ones. "I'm sorry. I wasn't expecting anyone to get off," she explained in a subdued voice. She dropped her gaze and tried to step back, only to be stopped by his arms still in place around her body. "Will you let go of me, Mr. Langdon?" she asked in an angry voice.

"Only if you say please," he answered, his amusement at her embarrassing predicament plainly obvious.

She clenched her fists in frustration, but something in the depths of his laughing gaze warned her not to push him. "Please," she muttered stonily, longing to slap his arrogant face.

"That's better," he murmured seductively, "but not quite sincere enough. "Maybe you can convince me that you really mean it." His eyes were like deep dark pools as he scanned the delicate beauty of her face.

Before Leslie could marshall her thoughts into a scathing put-down, she saw Cord's mouth headed in slow descent on a direct course with her own. For the first time in a long time—no, for the first time ever—

she found herself caught up in a maelstrom of feeling that threatened her very existence.

Her survival instincts were heightened by this invasion, urging with all their might for Leslie to bring a halt to this charade. But something else, a primeval urge, took over. She wanted him to touch her, wanted the intermingling of his scent with hers.

When the feather-light touch came, it seared Leslie's skin with flame that raced from her toes to the very ends of her hair. She was only vaguely aware of Cord shifting one arm so that it cradled her neck, the other clasping her body to his warm one. The exquisite hesitancy with which his lips hovered over her own brought an urgency to Leslie's being that had her straining toward him.

Her unexpected capitulation had almost as stunning an effect on Cord. He lifted his head fractionally to gaze in a bemused fashion at Leslie's face. Thick gold-tipped lashes brushed the delicate curve beneath her eyes, her cheeks an attractive shade of pink. But it was the inviting softness of her slightly parted lips that caused his breath to catch in his throat.

His mouth took hers again, this time hungrily, no longer searching or tentatively seeking. He inhaled her sweet intoxicating scent, tasted the inner softness of her mouth. His tongue was relentless in its quest.

Leslie was powerless to stem the response as she felt the tip of Cord's tongue withdraw and then begin a delicate tracing of the outline of her lips.

Each new assault brought with it an awakening of senses she'd thought safely submerged. She was caught in a state of timelessness, aware only of the magic he was creating, adding her own shy tasting, nibbling unthinkingly.

It was Cord's ragged breathing, his hoarsely muttered "I knew I wasn't wrong about you" that brought Leslie plummeting back to harsh reality with fatal surety.

Pride . . . and an inexplicable state of confusion left her momentarily bereft of speech. Her initial instinct regarding Cord had been more than correct. He was dangerously threatening and most humiliating of all, he knew it.

With a carefully contrived gesture of calmness Leslie drew herself upright from the intimate closeness of Cord's body, her hands braced against the muscles of his arms. "May I please leave now?" Her voice was barely audible in the quiet of the corridor.

She kept her eyes pinned on the buttons of the snowy white shirt Cord was wearing. At that moment nothing on earth could induce her to meet his knowing gaze.

Cord released her somewhat reluctantly, his hands sliding down her arms, while his piercing gaze searched out each feature of her face as if committing it to memory. "That was nicely done, Miss Garrison." He released her and stepped back, one long finger touching the tip of her nose. "Don't look so cross; it causes lines. I don't like my women to have lines."

It was on the tip of her tongue to remind him that she wasn't one of his women and that she had no desire to be, when he looked past her and smiled. "Hello, George. I was just on my way to see you when I ran into Miss Garrison." He switched from the devastating devil of only moments ago to a smiling, polite stranger.

George Corstairs came to a stop by Leslie, one arm dropping across her shoulders in an innocent fashion. "I'm glad to see you two getting along so well. Knowing your dislike for reporters, I was afraid you would give Leslie a bad time of it."

"Nonsense, George. Miss Garrison made the session so enjoyable I've been racking my brain to come up with something else newsworthy," he solemnly announced.

Leslie smiled sweetly at Cord. "Thank you, Mr. Langdon. But I'm sure that if you honor us with your charming presence for any length of time, there'll be numerous affairs to report." She turned on her heel and marched toward the door that led to the stairs, Cord Langdon's laughter filling the corridor with its hateful sound.

She hurried down the stairs and out of the building, her face flushed from her encounter with her tormentor. Damn him! He was the most insufferable devil she'd ever met.

The trip to her apartment was made in record

time, her anger causing her to disregard the speed limit. After parking her car and turning off the engine, Leslie slumped forward and rested her forehead on the steering wheel in anger and frustration.

She wasn't some naive young girl ready to withdraw at the slightest advance from a man. But every fiber of her being warned her against Cord Langdon, and for every warning there was an equally strong desire surfacing to taunt her, egging her on, urging her to take a chance.

She forced herself to move. After removing the keys from the ignition, she picked up her handbag and walked toward her apartment. Once inside, she headed for the small compact kitchen and fixed herself a drink. She carried it with her to the bathroom and sipped on it while she waited for the tub to fill.

Leslie sighed and stretched in the warm water, feeling some of the strain and tension of the day leave her body. As she rested her head back against the tub, she set her mind to the immediate problem of what to wear that evening. For some unaccountable reason she wanted to look especially nice. For whom? she asked herself, but it was a question that required no answer.

In the back of her mind stood one man, the silent mockery in his craggy face reminding her of her inability to thrust him aside as she'd done all the other men since her divorce. She could still feel the hardness of his chest against her breasts, his strong hands as they slid down her arms. She raised her arms and stared at them curiously, surprised to see that they didn't bare some mark from his touch. He didn't fit into her tame zoo as Miriam had called the various men she'd dated. But Leslie knew he was a force that sooner or later she would be compelled to deal with. In her heart she knew he was trouble, but she also knew he wasn't the sort one swept beneath the carpet and forgot.

Full rein was given to her thoughts, remembering his incredible maleness, the way he had raked her body with his searing gaze. *You'd be wise, my girl, to steer clear of him,* a tiny voice urged. *I'll try,* she promised, *I'll really try.* But for some reason the silent avowal lacked conviction.

As she dressed, Leslie remembered the letter from her dad that had been in the mail. A pang of guilt shot through her as she realized she hadn't called or visited him in a number of weeks. But, she reflected, he was a stubborn cuss, much the same as his daughter. She knew he was having trouble with his wife, Monica. She also knew he wouldn't welcome any comments from his daughter or anyone else.

Leslie stepped into her pale green dress and gently drew it over her hips and up to her shoulders. It clung to the slim curves of her body with just the proper suggestion of seduction, hinting at, but not completely molding each line of, her slender form. The plunging V of the neckline was the only revealing part of the dress, baring the shadowy valley between her creamy breasts.

She stepped back from the full-length mirror and critically viewed her reflection. "Not bad, Miss Garrison, not bad." She spoke out loud, giving a nodding moue of satisfaction. She walked over to the dressing table and selected a particular scent and applied a touch to her wrists and behind each ear. By the time Jeremy arrived, she was ready, impatient to be on her way.

Upon entering her apartment he eyed her dress with a devilish leer and made a comment that, coming from anyone else, would have infuriated her.

"One can always tell when you've been denied your little pleasures, Jer. You begin to take on the traits of a lecherous old man," she countered, and then laughed at the look of mock outrage that overtook his face.

"Lecherous old man? In that dress, Leslie, you could cause a saint to have second thoughts." He peered at the plunging V with a shake of his head. "I would strongly advise using a pin or two. Or"—he struggled to keep a straight face—"don't dare bend over."

She merely gathered up her handbag and the light wrap. "All right, Jer, are we even?"

He grinned. "Maybe. Let's get going. I'm all for getting through early and leaving."

Leslie laughed and followed him to the door. "Patience, my man, patience."

Nothing had been spared in the landscaping of the grounds, Leslie noted, as they swept up the circular drive directly in front of the entrance to the ultramodern structure. Stately palms swayed in the breeze, lush specimens of some of the twenty or so varieties that thrive so well in Florida. A row of hibiscus flanked each side of the wide walk leading toward the entrance, their red and yellow blossoms brilliant against the velvet green of the lawn. In front of the hibiscus grew scarlet sage, poinsettias, and gloriosa double daisies.

The only discordant note in the setting in Leslie's opinion was the design of the building. To her, it resembled a giant mushroom. But then, she'd sat at her father's knee as a youngster and listened and watched as he'd shown her different designs and structures that pleased him. He was not a follower of the more modern lines that most young architects sought, preferring instead the blending of both worlds in his designs.

Leslie also shared his passion for restoring old houses and buildings. One of John Garrison's finest hours had been when he was asked to serve on a committee in preparation for the restoration of Williamsburg.

As they stepped from the car, Jeremy looked at the new building with a high degree of concentration. "Does it lift off at midnight?" he questioned with a perfectly straight face.

"Possibly, so let's get our work over with and leave," Leslie agreed.

Once inside, they found the place teeming with

people. For the next hour or so Leslie and Jeremy worked like Trojans. It was an endless task, having short conversations with different people and pointing out something or someone to Jeremy that needed photographing. People were always anxious to have their names and faces appear in *Preview,* so it necessitated a flair for diplomacy to keep everyone happy.

On the whole Leslie found the people to be nice— generous. Of course there were the occasional snobs that she was forced to deal with, but she was more than capable of holding her own.

It was while she was having a quiet and enjoyable chat with Mildred Browning, one of the organizers of the gala, and a very charming person, that Leslie felt the skin on the back of her neck begin to tingle. She turned her head slightly, but she was unable to see anyone that could account for the strange sensation. Then someone stepped aside and she found herself looking across the room and straight into the eyes of Cord Langdon.

They stared at each other for several seconds across the space that separated them. Leslie despised the traitorous thumping of her heart that began the moment she saw him. She remained impassive, refusing to allow the tiniest flicker of her true feelings to show in her expression.

He was, without a doubt, the most striking man in attendance. In fact, if she were called on to describe him, she would be forced to lean more toward rough-hewn. Even in the casual manner in which he was leaning against the large desklike object, he exuded an air of forcefulness that was lacking in the other men in the same group.

During her unconscious scrutiny of him, he raised one eyebrow mockingly. It was only when he lifted his drink in silent greeting that Leslie was aware she had been staring.

Instead of giving in to the embarrassment she felt at having been caught, she lifted her chin and gave him a cheeky grin.

"Have you met Cord, Leslie?" Mildred asked, watching with amused interest the curious exchange between them.

"Yes, I have," she admitted, keeping her response cool and impersonal.

"He's an outrageous flirt, but I'm quite fond of him," the older woman replied.

*Who isn't?* Leslie thought with grim resignation. "Have you known him very long?"

"Oh, yes. Since he was a little boy." She gave a soft chuckle. "He only came this evening because I asked him. He hates affairs such as this." She gazed at the source of their conversation with fondness. "He's been on his own for so long, restrictions of any sort tend to stifle him."

"How well did you know his aunt?" Leslie asked curiously.

"Quite well. We were at school together, but we drifted apart in later years. She was a grasping, stingy woman. That is the reason Cord went away. She wanted to control his life, and he rebelled."

"Did he live with her?"

"Yes. His parents died when he was quite young. Agatha wasn't the most affectionate person in the world. I often wished I could have taken him, but as his only living relative she assumed the responsibility. It's a shame she had to wait until her death to show him any sort of kindness. They could have had some wonderful times together."

"But she did leave her estate to him." Leslie pointed out.

"That's true, but I'm afraid it was a little too late. That was the only gesture of love she ever made. I understand he's giving the entire inheritance to charity."

"It's a beautiful old place," said Leslie, refraining from discussing the article. "It's rather sad to think of its being deserted by the one remaining member of the family."

"Perhaps, but it was never a happy place for him." She smiled at Leslie. "How about you, my dear, have you gotten back in the swing of things since you've been back? We must seem quite tame after your stay in Chicago."

"Not at all. Of the two places I definitely prefer Miami. As to your other question, yes. George and Miriam have been most supportive. They've made the transition extremely easy for me."

"How are you, Mildred—Miss Garrison?" The

voice was deep, and Leslie would have known it anywhere in the world.

"I'm fine, Cord," Mildred answered. "Why don't you take Leslie over and get her something to eat? I see someone I must speak with."

She left them, leaving Leslie with the unpleasant feeling of a Christian being thrown to the lions. She drew a deep breath and raised her eyes to his face.

Cord was watching her with the same devilish grin on his face that she'd seen once before. "Shall we do as Mildred suggested?" he asked when Leslie thought the silence would never be broken.

"Thank you, but I've already had something. Tell me, Mr. Langdon, what brings you out this evening. Are you a patron of the arts as well?"

He laughed softly, looking around for an ashtray before he spoke. "Actually, I'm not, other than when Mildred puts the bite on me, which she does regularly." He let his gaze sweep over the large crowd of people, leaving Leslie with the distinct feeling that he would rather be someplace else at the moment. "To be quite honest, I hadn't planned on coming this evening until Mildred told me that your magazine would be covering it. When I learned that you would be here, I accepted her kind invitation."

"Most resourceful, Mr. Langdon," she replied, tipping her head in amusement at his outrageous flattery. Oh, he was smooth . . . too smooth to suit her.

"Don't you think we could dispense with the formalities? If you'll call me Cord, I'll call you Leslie. I don't think old George will mind, do you?"

*Not at all,* she wanted to shriek. She shuddered to think what that individual would do if he were present.

"Did you come alone?" he asked.

"No, I'm with Jeremy Keyes." She laughed. "As usual, he's off somewhere with his camera."

"As soon as you're through here, let's go somewhere and have a drink," he suggested.

Leslie was in a state of awareness where every incident was like watching actors perform on stage. From the hair on her head to each extremity of her body coursed a warmth that was almost frightening in its intensity. "I'm sorry," she replied in a quiet voice, "but I'm afraid I can't."

She wanted to go, wanted to learn more about this man. But something held her back, made her wary. For with all her ability to deal with the adversities that had been dealt her, she was vulnerable.

She'd thought her Achilles heel perfectly hidden, and at such time when she felt she was ready to love again, she could let her defenses down. But Cord Langdon was threatening those defenses as surely as if war had been declared between them.

He regarded her for a moment before speaking. "Do you have a date?"

"No," she answered honestly. "But we'll be quite late finishing up here, and I have a difficult day tomorrow."

His dark head bent to inspect the gold watch on his tanned wrist. "I didn't realize you were required to spend such long hours at your job. As one of the stockholders in *Preview* I must remember to question the policy that requires such long hours." He watched her, one brow raised in lazy assessment of the flush that slowly stole over her face.

"How nice, Mr. L—Cord. I'm sure all the employees of the magazine will appreciate your benevolent gesture," she replied. So that accounted for the royal treatment from George. No wonder he'd been so adamant in his instructions not to pry.

The amusement was wiped from his face to be replaced with a shrewd and thoughtful expression. "It won't work, Leslie. At the moment you've outfoxed me, but I've never been known to quit once something interested me, and you do. So be warned —this in no way settles our little problem. There's something about you that keeps pulling at me. I can't let it drop. I'll be getting in touch with you." He turned and walked away, leaving Leslie with conflicting emotions. She longed to rush after him, and yet she was afraid of the consequences if she gave in to such an impulsive urge.

After Cord left, the remainder of the evening seemed to drag interminably. By the time Leslie cornered Jeremy and asked him to take her home, her head was splitting. Whether from the noise of the party or from frustration, she wasn't sure.

Long after she was back at her apartment and in

bed, she remembered the warning Cord had given her and the fire of excitement that had shone in his eyes. Why now? Why at this precise moment in her life when she was still licking the wounds inflicted from her last emotional battle?

Damn! It wasn't fair. She silently railed and ranted against the dark image of the man who had come to dominate completely her thoughts and mind. *Don't be such a nerd,* the tiny voice she was beginning to hate urged. *You've never been such a coward. It's not like you to shrink from a challenge. Always playing safe can insure you of some lonely years to come.*

But Cord was only looking for a brief respite from whatever it was that bored men in his lofty position. Was she ready for a quick affair that would be over almost before it began? Why not?

No, no, and a thousand times no! Yet, after finally giving in to and floating in the arms of Morpheus, her mouth curved in a soft smile as she dreamed. The sight of Cord's considerably large frame stretched out amid a field of daisies while she sat close by his side and fashioned a crown of the delicate flowers seemed so real. She leaned over him, her breasts pressing against the firmness of his broad chest, and placed the crown on his dark head, a tiny grin on her face.

The flowers were lost in the slight scuffle that ensued. Their positions were quickly reversed and Leslie found herself beneath him, the deep throb of desire springing up in her as his lips covered hers.

## CHAPTER FOUR

Leslie awoke from her night's sleep with the disposition of a bear with a sore head. She staggered toward the bathroom with her eyes only half opened. Once there she fumbled with the knobs on the sink until the cool water was running. After splashing her face repeatedly she was relieved to see that her eyes *could* open to their normal size.

After brushing her teeth and combing her hair, she went to the kitchen and started the coffee. She slipped some bread into the toaster and poured a glass of orange juice. While waiting for the coffee to perk, she remembered the letter from her dad.

After finding it among the stack of mail that was on the desk in the living room, Leslie went back to the kitchen and poured herself a cup of coffee and settled down to give the letter her full attention.

Her dad's habit of hastily scribbling a line or two and shooting it off to her was a carryover from her college days. It was a practice he'd continued over the years. He telephoned as well, but Leslie could expect a short note at least every two weeks.

While she sipped her coffee and munched on a piece of toast, she scanned the rather lengthy missive, surprised at the two pages. There was nothing earth-shattering, but from what she read between the lines left Leslie with the distinct impression that the situation between her dad and Monica was fast approaching a showdown.

Monica had never been openly hostile toward Leslie, but a cold war existed between the two women. Leslie knew her stepmother had married her dad simply as a means of removing herself from the rat race of having to work and support herself.

John Garrison had been quite vulnerable after his wife's death, and Monica, his secretary for a number of years, lost no time in insinuating herself into his personal life.

Leslie had often wondered how a man as intelligent and successful as her dad could have been taken in by such an obvious gold digger. Had it not been for Nellie, the staunch housekeeper of many years, Leslie probably wouldn't have stayed as close as she had.

She read the letter through again before putting it aside. If he needed her, she would go. Otherwise she felt it best to let him work it out in his own way. But she would go home for a weekend in the near future.

It was while she was straightening the kitchen and rinsing out the few dishes she'd used that the dream she'd had the night before came to mind.

Leslie stood as though paralyzed. My God, she thought to herself, her mind performing beautifully in the process of total recall. The picture of Cord Langdon "reposing" amid a field of daisies was the most comical thing she could imagine. Heavens! She would never be able to look him in the eye again and not see a crown of flowers encircling his head.

Perhaps there was something to be said for the meaningless affairs a number of women indulged in. After all, when one started having such idiotic dreams as she'd had, something was definitely out of whack.

Once at the office Leslie threw herself into her work with a sigh of relief. The fast and demanding pace was what was needed to help keep her mind off Cord.

Miriam was curious about the museum gala, and Leslie found herself relating incidents from the evening. "From all accounts it was a huge success," Leslie told her.

"Mildred called this morning to thank us for the excellent job you and Jeremy did in covering the event," Miriam informed her.

"If everyone were as nice as she is, our jobs would

be incredibly easy. By the way, Cord Langdon was there."

Miriam glanced at Leslie and then returned to studying the typewritten account of the evening. "And?" she asked, not sure just what Leslie had in mind.

"And," she shrugged, "he was attractive as sin, as usual, and he asked me out for a drink."

"Did you accept?"

"No."

"Oh, Leslie. Why not?" Miriam asked in an exasperated tone. She was tempted to shake her young assistant.

"Pure unadulterated fear." She leaned forward and placed her elbows on the desk and rested her chin in her hands. "I know it sounds stupid, Miriam, but I feel threatened by him." She had to laugh at the shocked expression that registered on Miriam's face. "No, no, not physically. After all, I'm not your average pocket-sized female. It's emotionally. And when I read or hear of his past exploits with women, I can't help but compare him with Charles."

"That's understandable, I suppose," Miriam admitted. "But for some reason, I think you're wrong. Oh, I'm not saying he hasn't played around. But underneath that devil-may-care attitude I think he has some very definite ideas about life. And, of course, I don't need to point out his fantastic success in the business world."

"No, but I know from past experience that a jaded

personal life can go hand in hand with a successful career. I suppose it comes down to what one terms success." She gave a quick grin. "I sound as though I thoroughly disapprove of him, don't I?"

"Well, I don't think you'd be exactly welcomed to offer a testimonial in his behalf."

"Just between you and me, Miriam, I find him the most attractive man I've ever known." She spread her hands in a gesture of confusion. "As to the outcome, I can't say. After last night he might let the matter drop and all I'll have will be a few memories. Who knows?"

"I wish I could help you, honey, but I'm afraid Charles did such an excellent job on you, only time can do that. But you mustn't allow the past to cloud the future. There are good men to be had." She sighed deeply. "Don't do as I've done, Leslie. I wanted so badly to succeed in what I considered a man's world, that I let life slip by. There's many a time that I'd gladly give it all up just to have a son or daughter call and say they're coming to see me or know the joy of feeling the chubby arms of grandchildren around my neck." There was a suspicious glitter in her eyes, and Leslie quickly looked away.

"I'm sorry, Miriam, I had no idea you felt this way," she replied huskily. "You've always seemed so happy."

"Of course," she declared, a hint of asperity in her voice. "Can you imagine the looks of pity that would be leveled toward me if everyone knew?" She shook her head. "No, I couldn't bear that. The only reason I'm telling you is that I see so much of myself in you. You have strong leadership qualities, Leslie, and that's good. You're stubborn and strong-willed, as you need to be for this business. But don't make the mistake of settling for those qualities you possess in place of a home and children."

Leslie dropped her gaze to her hands, giving Miriam time to compose herself. Peeking into the heart of someone close was not a very enjoyable thing.

She'd been back at her desk only a short time when the telephone rang. Leslie reached for the receiver with one hand, her mind and eyes on the story she was working on. "Leslie Garrison, may I help you?"

"Hello, Leslie. This is Cord Langdon. Have I interrupted something or can you talk?"

She sat back in her chair, a mixture of excitement and apprehension attacking her body. "I can spare a few minutes, Cord. What can I do for you?" she asked.

"Do you have plans for lunch?"

"No, I've no plans."

"Would you consider eating with me? Before you get ready to refuse, I promise to have you back on time."

*Why not?* she asked herself. *Surely I can withstand an hour in his company without suffering permanent damage.* "I'd like that," she quickly answered before her better judgment asserted itself. "Where shall I meet you? It'll be difficult finding a parking space close to my office."

"No problem. I'm putting to use the office George offered me, so I'll stop by for you," he assured her.

As soon as she was through talking with him, Leslie dialed Carol's number. When she answered, Leslie explained that she wouldn't be able to have lunch with her. They made a date for the following day and Leslie hung up.

Leslie spent the hour before the lunch date on the list of things that George had asked her to take care of. Mainly it involved making several telephone calls, and she was just finishing up with the last one when she looked up and discovered Cord leaning against the door frame watching her. She smiled and waved him to the chair by her desk and went on with her conversation. Strangely enough, there was none of the nervous, jittery feeling that had assailed her when first meeting him. Mentally she congratulated herself on advancing forward to a degree and was able to deal with the annoying woman on the other end of the phone with a bit more consideration than she really felt.

"Problems?" Cord asked, once she'd replaced the receiver. He'd been listening and could see that Leslie had almost gritted her teeth to keep from telling the woman where to go!

"You could say that," she ruefully admitted. "I should be used to her by now, but she never fails to surprise me with her incredible gall. I've never met anyone pushing so hard to become accepted by the local grande dames of society." She glanced at her watch. "I'm sorry, I've kept you waiting."

"Think nothing of it. We'll simply add a few minutes to our lunch."

Leslie grabbed her purse and then scooted over to tell Miriam that she was leaving.

During the ride down in the elevator, Cord kept a steady flow of small talk going. Leslie found herself watching him and listening to him with a calmness that surprised even her. He was dressed in a dark suit, white shirt, and dark tie—the epitome of the successful executive.

It took little to visualize him chairing a meeting of the board or rapping out decisions in staccatolike fashion. But why did he choose to lead such an aimless personal life?

They settled on a small restaurant near the office. For some unaccountable reason, Leslie preferred it to one of the fancier places. After they'd given their orders to the waitress, Cord leaned back in his chair, his gaze openly admiring his companion. Her auburn hair, falling softly to her shoulders with a casual flip at the ends, the green eyes that met his without a hint of guile in them, and on to the attractive green dress she wore.

"Tell me, Leslie, are you one of the new breed of women that has sprung up, bent on a career to the exclusion of everything else?"

"To be quite honest, I haven't seen anything as

attractive as my work. It's taken me awhile to get where I am, and I'm afraid I'm not anxious to give it up." Typical, she was thinking. Like most men, he regarded her career as nothing compared to being a wife. "Don't you think women are as capable of handling responsible positions as men?" she asked, a gleam of mischief in her eyes.

He shrugged, a smile tugging at the corners of his mouth. "Of course. I know several women that fit the bill perfectly. But on the other hand, they're not exactly what I'd call your average soft feminine woman."

Leslie leaned forward, ready to defend her stand with vigor. "But that's just the point, Cord. They don't want to be considered soft powderpuffs. They want to be appreciated for their intelligence and how well they do the job," she pointed out.

He didn't answer, for the waitress chose that moment to bring their orders. After she was gone, Cord asked, "Are you saying they don't want marriage and children? That they're only concerned with showing the world how brilliant they are?" He shook his head. "Somehow you don't strike me as being that way at all. Others perhaps, but not you. You're a warm, vital person and I find it difficult to believe that your are content to report on other people's parties and weddings when you could easily be hosting your own." A measure of displeasure had crept into his voice, and the pleasant expression on his face had been replaced by a scowl.

"Well." Leslie lifted her shoulders indifferently. "You're definitely in the majority with your thinking. I hate to disillusion you, but I'm perfectly content. Being attached to one man can become quite boring," she replied airily.

He was silent for a moment, his attention seemingly devoted to the excellent quiche he'd ordered. "So, Leslie Garrison, the successful young journalist, also plays the field." He subjected her to a searching gaze, his expression unreadable. "I'm surprised that you can manage such a full professional and personal career," he remarked acidly.

"Really? Has that same problem proved difficult for you, Cord?" she asked sweetly.

His displeasure was evident by the tightly drawn line of his lips. "No, it damn well hasn't, Miss Garrison," he snapped in a controlled voice, his eyes like chips of ice.

By then Leslie's sense of humor asserted itself, and she was finding it difficult not to laugh. "Oh, dear, I've offended you. I see I'm back to being Miss Garrison." She took her time adding the proper amount of sugar to her coffee. "What's that old saying, Cord? 'What's sauce for the goose is . . .'" She left the sentence unfinished.

"I'm well aware of the old saying, Leslie, but I fail to see how it applies to me. Please, elaborate."

"It's quite simple. You refuse to accept the fact that a woman can be successful at her job and be a wife and mother at the same time. And heaven forbid

71

if she should decide in favor of a career. In your opinion only a sexless prude can carry on in this man's world." She stopped the lengthy attack only long enough to take a sip of coffee. She was unaware of the extra sparkle in her eyes or the heightened color of her cheeks.

Cord had leaned back and was watching her with a gleam of admiration that would have surprised her had she been in the proper frame of mind to appreciate it.

"I'm curious about something, Cord. Have you taken out, socially, any of the women that you say do such a fantastic job for you in your organization?"

Cord's face turned a peculiar shade of red as at that moment he sipped his coffee. Then, rather hastily, he placed the cup in the saucer. "There's no way. I'd have to be out of my mind."

Leslie leaned back, her elbows resting on the arms of her chair, her hands opened in an expressive gesture. "There. I rest my case."

"Well, don't plan on a lengthy nap. First of all, I have three very efficient ladies in my employ. And in spite of your biased opinion of most male employers, I've seen to it that promotions and raises were given on individual merit, not the sex of the employee. Second, are the ladies themselves. One of them is old enough to be my mother. Another is not inclined to favor the male sex." He gave her a very pointed look. "Do I make myself clear?" At her grudgingly given nod he went on. "That leaves one. She is not the type

I'd consider escorting to dinner other than from a purely friendly gesture. She tips the scales at two hundred pounds. Her mind and soul may be as beautiful as paradise and as restful as a Scottish glen, but I'm simply not interested."

*Oh, you rat fink, you wiggled out of that easily enough,* Leslie thought to herself. "You're to be commended for your fairness, Cord," she said instead.

"Thank you, Leslie. Your kindness overwhelms me," he replied solemnly, struggling to keep from laughing.

They were both fencing, and Cord was well aware of the no-trespassing attitude emanating from Leslie. But they were two equally stubborn people, and the desire to know each other better had been decided the moment they met. And while Cord was the very image of success—the supposed answer to every young woman's dream, Leslie was his counterpart.

Her experience with Charles Brien had brought about a maturity that, coupled with her inborn common sense, had produced a young woman with tremendous ability and a rare gift for meeting life and its challenges head-on.

They were both silent for several seconds, each undoubtedly weighing the other—planning the strategy for the next skirmish. For it had to come as surely as the sun rose in the morning and set in the evening.

After that slight go at each other, they resumed eating—and a less lively conversation. Leslie gleaned a small amount of information that had been missing from the file she'd studied before meeting him. The most interesting thing being his genuine fondness for children.

"Is that really why you gave the estate to the Leher Foundation?" she asked.

Cord smiled. "Did you doubt my motives?"

"Well . . ." she hedged. "All right, I did question it. For a while I wondered if you were trying to ingratiate yourself with the local political figures," she confessed.

He stared incredulously before laughing . . . and laughing. Leslie bristled like an angry kitten at his cavalier treatment. Cord composed himself, his rough features noticeably softened by his humor. "I'm sorry, Leslie, but you have the damnedest way of going right to the heart of the matter." He shook his head. "It's probably one of the few completely unselfish gestures I've made in years. Everyone, with the exception of one suspicious redhead, thinks it's great. I can see that our relationship will be interesting, to say the least."

Leslie eyed him dispassionately across the small table. "Our relationship, Cord?" she asked pointedly.

"Yes, Leslie. Our relationship. And to cause that faint heart of yours to beat even more erratically, I'll say this—I don't play by the rules."

Leslie was silent as his gaze held hers. The gauntlet had been thrown down in plain view. She could either accept the challenge or pretend an asinine indifference that would immediately cast her in the role of fool.

"That's just as well, for I'm wary of men who present a polished image to the public and hide their true colors underneath. I play cagey as well. And"—she spoke softly—"I like my freedom and independence."

## CHAPTER FIVE

When Cord left her at her office there was no mention of another date. But Leslie knew she would be seeing Cord again. After all, there was a lot to be said for a man who could retain his masculinity while wearing a crown of daisies.

Miriam was at Leslie's desk, talking on the phone and scribbling in a hurried fashion on a pad. Leslie put away her things and walked over to the desk and glanced down at the notes.

The underlined name of Paul Papolous stood out. She placed her forefinger by the name and looked questioningly at Miriam. The latter shook her head. "All right, George, we'll get right on it." She replaced the receiver and slipped her gold earring back on her right ear. "How was lunch?"

Leslie unconsciously fingered the narrow gold bracelets on her left arm, giving Miriam a saucy grin. "The food was delicious."

"And the escort?"

Leslie shrugged, and then walked around the desk and sat down. "I really can't see what all the fuss is about," she replied innocently, her eyes dancing at the sight of Miriam's increased agitation.

"I just bet you can't. Apparently from the rosy glow in your cheeks, you enjoyed yourself," she sniffed.

"Oh, Miriam, I'm only teasing." She was quiet for a moment, giving careful consideration to her next words. "I enjoyed being with him. He's vital, stimulating. I think I understand the reason why he's so sought after. But he is opinionated. Especially regarding women and careers."

"Are you seeing him again?" Miriam asked.

"Perhaps. Who knows? At the moment I have a mountain of work and a long list of parties to attend. I'll have to put Cord Langdon on hold."

Miriam closed her eyes and slowly shook her head. "Oh, to be young and indifferent again."

"By the way, can I possibly get off a couple of hours early this afternoon? I must get some shopping done, my cupboard is bare."

"Oh, dear." Miriam looked at the pad in her hand and then back at Leslie. "How about taking some time off now, and then go with Jeremy this evening? I know it's short notice, but I'm going to be out as well, and George wants someone to look in on this affair."

Immediately, Leslie saw her one free evening going out the window. "All right," she said resignedly. "But what about Susan? Can't she take over for this evening?"

Miriam shook her head. "You know George. He doesn't think she's ready. Besides, the party is being given by Lila Ames, and you know how fond she is of you. If you'll do this, you can come in at noon tomorrow."

"I detest people who accept bribes, Miriam," Leslie grinned impishly. "But, I'll take it. Would you care to make it a full day?"

"No, I would not."

"Oh, well, no harm in asking. Now tell me something about this evening and"—she reached for the pad in Miriam's hand and checked the name—"Mr. Papolous? Any relation to the shipping magnate?"

"He *is* the shipping magnate. He and a brother were partners. The brother died, so he's been running the show for a couple of years. George got wind of his being in town to meet with some people—something to do with the shipping of oil from Alaska to Mexico. Don't worry about the technical side, Ted Bates is back from London and he'll try to get an interview later on as to the real reason he's here. You and Jeremy just do your usual thing."

Leslie started to turn away when a frown came to her smooth forehead. "Miriam?" Her voice was full of question. "This isn't another of George's little tricks, is it? He hasn't decided he'd like to see me basking in the sun on some Greek island, has he?"

"No, no. Be serious, Leslie," her boss snapped. "This is strictly business. Paul Papolous is news wherever he goes. And so far none of the other magazines have learned that he's here. Lila and Ray are close friends, so there's been no publicity."

"Yes, ma'am."

"I'm sorry, but things seem to be piling up on me. If I occasionally bark, forgive," the older woman apologized.

"Bark away, I'll survive. By the way, how old is this character?"

Miriam frowned. "Early fifties—very distinguished. I've pulled his file, but there's not much to see. He avoids or suppresses, when he can, most publicity. And if he chooses to do the same now, we'll cooperate. After all, it never hurts to keep on the good side of people in his circle."

"In other words, I'm not to pry. All right, I get the picture."

After Miriam had gone, Leslie opened the file and studied it carefully. For all the information it revealed, Paul Papolous might have been a monk. It gave an approximate estimate of his wealth, causing Leslie's eyes to stretch to an incredible width. It was positively indecent.

There was a daughter and no mention of his wife, so one could only assume he had been widowed or divorced. Reading further, she learned he was living apart from his wife.

She closed the folder and leaned back in her chair, her mind already taken up with the mystery of the wealthy tycoon and his peculiar marital status. Greeks were notoriously straitlaced when it came to their wives. While a man might have a mistress tucked away, his wife had to be as pure as the driven snow. Had the poor thing slipped? *If she did, I hope she enjoyed it,* Leslie thought, *because she'll probably have to make the memory last a lifetime.*

With a sigh she closed the folder and began her shopping list—mushrooms, celery, green peppers—the list went on. By the time it was completed, Leslie eyed it skeptically. She might have to float a check. She leaned back in her chair and stared out the window. *I wonder what Cord's favorite dish is?* she thought. A cozy picture of the two of them flooded her thoughts. She could see herself adding the finishing touches to dinner while Cord poured the wine. There would be soft music in the background and candles on the table. She would be wearing some soft, clinging gown, and when he took her in his arms and kissed her . . . Suddenly the ridiculousness of where her thoughts were leading to hit Leslie. She did a swift check to make sure Miriam wasn't watching her and drew a sigh of relief when she saw that no one had witnessed her dreamy expression. She placed her palms to her warm cheeks and slowly shook her head. *I've got to snap out of this,* she scolded herself.

*I'm becoming obsessed with Cord Langdon.* She quickly gathered up her shopping list and handbag and left the office.

When the doorbell pealed at exactly eight o'clock that evening, Leslie lost no time in answering. Friend or no, Jeremy was the most impatient man of her acquaintance. She hurried across the room and opened the door with a flourish, a silly grin on her face.

"Do you always answer the door in such a friendly manner?" Ted Bates asked, his blond brows raised in fiendish delight at her discomfiture. "May I come in? I'm taking Jeremy's place."

Leslie lifted her chin haughtily as she groped for a suitable remark to cut him down to size. Ted wasn't her favorite person. He'd laid siege with a determined effort when Leslie first returned to the magazine. But when she grew tired of his blatant attempts to get her into his bed, she stopped seeing him. Thinking himself to be irresistible, he'd never quite gotten over the putdown.

"Of course, Ted." She stepped back. "But I'm ready if you are. Miriam suggested we get there around eight thirty."

He snorted derisively, his handsome face taking on a sneering look. "By all means, let's get right to it." He flicked off the switch by the door that controlled two of the lamps in the living room and held open the door. "Never let it be said that I kept Miss Garrison from her job."

Leslie couldn't resist a tiny dig as she walked past him. She reached out and patted his cheek. "Now, now, Ted. Don't be so nervous. Anyone would think this is your first big break." She ignored the murderous look he threw her, thinking what a pompous ass he really was.

For the most part the drive was made in silence. Each attempt by Leslie at conversation was met with a curt rebuff. They were on the MacArthur Causeway that spanned Biscayne Bay before Ted could bring himself to speak. "I hope they warned you not to try for an interview," he said somewhere between a grunt and a growl.

Leslie glanced at him for a moment, wondering how he'd gotten as far as he had, in view of his insufferable ego. "Don't be stupid, Ted. Of course I've been warned. I'm aware of the vast difference in our respective fields, but some of the basic rules still apply. By the way, why the switch with Jeremy?"

"It seemed pointless for all three of us to come, and there was some to-do at the yacht club involving the regatta that he had to cover. He would have been useless anyway," he added in a dismissive tone, at which Leslie took immediate umbrage.

"Jeremy, useless? He could go to any wire service or magazine tomorrow and you know it."

"All right, he's great. Does that make you happy?" he snipped, his mood even uglier than before. "But genius or not, this Greek has to be handled with kid gloves. George wants this scoop, so it will have to be done carefully. Since you know the people giving the party, it's a perfect cover for me to sniff around."

Leslie grimaced slightly. "I suppose it is, but it's occasions such as this that I dislike. I prefer being open with people."

"In the social end you can, but in my position it's dog-eat-dog. Besides, if Paul Papolous is involved, you can bet it's big."

"Why does he and his wife live apart?"

Ted gave an indifferent shrug. "I'm not sure, but it's been that way for years. He's the original sphinx when it comes to maintaining silence."

He slowed the car and took the exit to Poincia Island. It was one of several manmade islands that flanked the causeway. In the distance could be seen the wrought iron gates that guarded the entrance to the Ames estate.

After parking the car, they were admitted by a smiling houseboy wearing a white jacket and dark trousers.

"Good evening, Raoul," Leslie greeted the young man. "How are you?"

His face broke into a big grin at the small gesture of friendliness. He bobbed his head up and down like a Yo-Yo. "Fine, Miss Garrison, fine."

"This is Mr. Bates, Raoul, a friend of mine." Ted was given the same smiling Yo-Yo greeting, and they moved on.

They were shown into a large room to the right of

the spacious foyer that had one entire wall given over to glass. The sheer white draperies, shot through with a gold thread, were open, as were the huge sliding glass doors. A mixture of teak, bamboo furniture, and glass-topped tables was scattered throughout the room, blending beautifully. There were huge plants adding their cooling effect to the surroundings.

The guests had spilled over to the deck where flaming flambeaus, placed at intervals, hinted at a Polynesian setting. It was very effective, thought Leslie, as she quickly scanned the sea of faces.

At that moment their hostess, Lila Ames, saw them and came rushing over, the soft green folds of her dress flowing out behind her. "Leslie, how nice. I was afraid you weren't going to make it," she exclaimed, giving her a quick kiss on the cheek. She turned and smiled at Ted.

"Lila Ames meet Ted Bates, a friend of mine." Lila was obviously quite taken with Ted's flashy good looks, so Leslie was relieved of a tiny bit of guilt at bringing him.

Lila caught Leslie watching the faces of the other guests and said, "Now, Leslie. Enjoy yourself for a change. There are several unattached males here, so circulate, kick up your heels."

Leslie gave her a teasing grin. "You mean you don't want me to mention anything at all about the beautifully planned party, the distinguished guest of honor, or name any of the people present?"

Lila looked at the tall, slim redhead, stunning in a creation of pinkish-biege, the fabric soft and clinging. "You know I'll kill you if there isn't some small mention, but as my friend I also expect you to forget your duties as a reporter and enjoy." She waved one arm in an expansive gesture. "There are some gorgeous men, darling."

Leslie couldn't help but grin at Ted's expression as Lila drew them into the throng and began introducing them. When their hostess had so easily discounted his presence as Leslie's escort, he'd been surprised. It was impossible for Leslie not to feel some delight at his obvious chagrin.

There were men, and each one seemed intent on granting Leslie's slightest wish. She absolutely glowed in the attention, laughing and easily parrying the good-natured joking. No one was out of line, it was simply a fantastic party with an abundance of good food and liquor, the latter accounting for a great deal of the lavishly spoken compliments paid Leslie and the other women as well.

After a while Leslie looked around for Ted, wondering where he'd gone off to. Was it possible that he'd cornered the guest of honor so quickly? Surely not. She turned back to two young men, each attempting to outdo the other in luring her away. She was laughing at some outrageous remark from one when a short, broad-shouldered man with iron-gray hair approached them.

Leslie's first impression was that he possessed one

85

of the strangest faces she'd ever seen. It was almost square, with a determined chin and full lips. His nose was equal to Jeremy's in size and shape. But it was his eyes that were his redeeming feature. They were like warm, brown pools, with incredibly thick lashes fringing them. His shaggy brows and high forehead completed the interesting picture.

He shouldered his short frame between the two younger men with an air of authority that brooked no argument. "Miss Garrison, I'm Paul Papolous." He extended a wide, short-fingered hand and Leslie unhesitatingly allowed hers to be caught in his warm clasp. "Let me take you away from these young Lochinvars." He waved a dismissive hand toward the two men. "They have no idea how to treat something as rare and beautiful as you." He tucked her hand in the curve of his arm as he walked her toward the deck.

Their exit was treated with derisive hoots by her two adoring swains. But her companion ignored them and smiled at her. "I hope I didn't interrupt anything important."

"No, not at all," she said smilingly. "But they were amusing. Lila always manages to give great parties, and her guests are enjoyable."

They had reached one of the low canvas-covered benches that were built along the sides of the deck. Paul removed a large white square from his inside jacket pocket and wiped away any hint of dust, and then indicated that Leslie should sit. He joined her and leaned back, giving a deep sigh of satisfaction. "Now"—he turned and let his eyes roam appreciatively over her amused face—"tell me something about yourself. I know that you're a reporter with *Preview,* but tell me about Leslie Garrison, the woman."

She smiled, completely bowled over by this little man with the gentle, ugly face. No one had warned her of his overwhelming personality. "I'm afraid I'm very ordinary. I enjoy my work, and I live alone. I like animals, children, and old houses." She tipped her head to one side and smiled. "Not very exciting, is it? Perhaps I should have embellished it slightly and said that I'm really on the trail of a top Russian double agent, and that I'm being kept by some important official in our government."

Her companion threw back his head and roared, his expression completely relaxed. After regaining his composure, he said, "Now I see why you're a success. You have a sense of humor as well as ability."

"Thank you," she answered, pleased by his words of praise.

"But tell me, does marriage and a family figure in your future?"

Leslie turned so that she could look out over the bay as well as face her companion. "Perhaps. I have been married, but it didn't work out." She met his steady gaze. "It tends to make one hesitant about trying again. But if you're asking me if I want a husband and children, then the answer is yes."

He smiled and patted her hand that was laying on the seat between them. "I'm glad. It would be a shame otherwise. You were made to warm some lucky man's bed and have his children."

"Someone else said almost the same thing to me today." A picture of Cord's face flashed before her eyes. She was unaware of the softness that had entered her voice as she spoke or the glow that came to her eyes.

"Is this someone very special?"

Leslie looked down at her hands for a moment before answering. "I'm afraid he could be," she murmured huskily.

"Why afraid?"

"I suppose I'm afraid of making another mistake," she confessed, not having the slightest problem in talking with this adorable man.

"So what?" he pointed out. "Nothing in life is certain. If you wait for a sure thing, you could grow old alone or become dreadfully bored with someone that you were sure fitted your role of perfection."

"Is that the same premise you apply in your business dealings?" she asked curiously.

"To a great extent, yes. To be successful one must take a chance. Is this man you refer to a success at what he's doing?"

"Oh, yes, remarkably so."

"Then go after him."

She laughed at his bluntness. "You make it sound so simple."

"Not simple, but there has to be a particular moment when one decides to withdraw or to forge ahead. Once that's done, the rest becomes easier." He reached into an inside pocket and removed a cigar. He looked questioningly at Leslie. At her nod he unwrapped it and lit it. After getting it going to his satisfaction, he said, "Now it's your turn."

She looked puzzled for a moment. "I'm sorry, but I don't follow you."

"Weren't you supposed to try to learn something about me? Well, go ahead. Ask me some questions." He adopted a crestfallen expression that was amusing. "Isn't there anything about me that your reporter's heart is longing to know?" he teased.

Leslie grinned. She'd been searching for a suitable opening, and here he was handing it to her. "There is one thing that puzzled me when I read the file on you. Why do you and your wife live apart?" It was one of the few times in her career when she was hesitant. She had no desire to alienate his positive feelings toward *Preview* nor did she want to turn the evening into a sort of press conference. But it was too great an opportunity to miss.

His luminous eyes stared at her for several seconds as if her question surprised him. "Is that all? Not why I'm here or how much I'm worth?"

"Your approximate worth was mentioned in the file and"—she gave him a pert grin—"I was suitably impressed. As to why you're here, that doesn't come under my particular job. Ted Bates, who came with me, is one of our top correspondents. He's hoping to get an interview with you."

"I see. So, you want to know why Maria and I live apart? We don't. She stays at our home on one of the Greek islands. I'm there as much as possible, which isn't as often as I like."

"Couldn't she travel with you?"

"She does occasionally, but she hates the crowds and the news media that always manage to cover our every move. My wife is a woman of very simple taste." He stared at Leslie for a moment. "She's also remarkably like you except for being a great deal older. She's tall, her curves a bit more voluptuous than yours, but by no means fat. Her long black hair is like a raven's wing with the sun shining on it. I worship her and would go to any length to protect her." He shook his head. "No, my dear, my Maria doesn't live apart from me. She's as vital to my existence as the very air I breathe."

"I'm glad. Somehow, after talking with you, my first impression seemed all wrong." She was thoughtful for a moment. "Is it all right with you if I mention something to the effect that you and she reside on an island off the coast of Greece?"

"Of course. I trust you to be discreet. I'll even allow your Mr. Bates a brief few minutes. By the way, is this man you're interested in as tall as a mountain, with dark hair and eyes?"

Leslie was slightly taken aback. "Why, yes, how did you know?"

"Well"—he folded his arms across his chest in a resigned manner—"he's been watching us for the past ten minutes and now he's headed this way with an angry glint in his eyes. I suggest we break up this enjoyable twosome before my aging body is flattened by your protector. Just one more word of advice, Leslie. I like the looks of him."

She barely heard these last words, for at his warning she'd swung around, only to encounter the stony gaze of Cord as he strode purposefully toward them.

Both Paul and Leslie stood, Paul's face smiling as he extended his hand and introduced himself. Cord acknowledged the introduction in a short, clipped manner, his eyes never leaving Leslie's face. For some strange reason she felt quite like a child with her hand caught in the cookie jar.

"Leslie, it's been a pleasure. I'll look forward to reading your account of this delightful evening." He turned to Cord. "Mr. Langdon." Then he left them, his generous mouth twitching with tightly controlled amusement.

For the first time in her adult life Leslie found herself in the unique position of being speechless. She reached out a tentative hand toward Cord and started to withdraw it when he grabbed it in a tight clasp. "Get your things; we're leaving." His lips were drawn in a tight line of suppressed violence.

"But . . . but I can't go right now, I'm supposed

to be working," she explained in a voice not quite steady. "Besides, I came with Ted Bates."

He drew her close to him none too gently, his hands gripping her upper arms. "Leslie, I'm not a patient man. You can either walk out or I'll carry you. Which is it to be?" he demanded in a low voice. She stared at the determined jaw, the muscles frozen taut. Her gaze moved upward to the burning glare of his eyes. She licked her lips in a nervous gesture. "I'll get my things and speak to Lila."

Cord stayed by her side as she made her excuses to her hostess. Lila's eyes went from Cord to Leslie, a perceptive gleam appearing as she took in Leslie's agitated state and Cord's angry countenance. "I understand perfectly, Leslie. I'm so glad you could make it. Give my regards to Miriam. You and Cord must come to dinner soon."

Leslie murmured that it would be nice, as Cord's hold on her arm tightened and he almost pushed her toward the door.

## CHAPTER SIX

Not a word was spoken as they walked to the car. A light breeze was blowing in off the bay, causing Leslie to shiver. Whether from the actual coolness of the evening or from apprehension, she wasn't sure. Cord transferred his hold from her elbow to her shoulder in silent concession. When they reached the car, he opened the door and waited until she was seated, and in seconds he was behind the wheel. The engine sprang to life and they sped down the driveway.

During the course of their hurried exit and the silent moments afterward, Leslie managed to calm the feeling of near panic that had first assailed her when she'd turned and saw Cord coming toward her. In its stead were the beginnings of a slow-burning anger, anger directed toward the man seated beside her and his indomitable will that brushed aside everything but his own wants and desires.

"Is it a darkly guarded secret, or am I allowed the privilege of asking where we're going?" she curtly inquired.

Cord turned and gave her an unreadable look before speaking. "To my place." The terse reply was further indication that his anger hadn't subsided at all.

"I see."

"No, I seriously doubt you do. But before the night's over you will."

"My, my. That certainly has ominous overtones. May I ask just why you're so angry? I know we disagreed on a number of things at lunch today, but it didn't seem to bother you then."

"All in good time, *Miss Garrison,* all in good time."

And with that, she had to be satisfied. But short of jumping from the speeding car, which would be completely idiotic, she had no recourse but to wait, albeit impatiently.

The remainder of the trip was made in strained silence. And while she had experienced anger only moments ago, there was also an air of mystery surrounding Cord's strange behavior.

The bright beam of the headlights caught and held the entrance to the drive to his home. He slowed the car down and made the turn. In seconds they were stopped in front of the gracious old house, its lines bathed in the softened glow of moonlight.

Without breaking his tight-lipped control, Cord got out of the car and came around to her side. He opened the door and offered Leslie his hand. She accepted it, finding his clasp infinitely warmer than his personality.

When they entered the dimly lit living room, Leslie gave him a quick look. "Is your housekeeper here?"

"No," he informed her. "We're all alone. Why?" He seemed unreasonably annoyed by her question.

She shrugged. "No reason, Cord. I was simply making conversation, that's all. Why so fractious? You've been in a foul mood ever since you got to Lila's. What's wrong?"

Cord ignored the question. He removed his jacket and tie, tossing them onto a chair. As he opened several buttons of his shirt, he said, "Make yourself comfortable"—he waved toward the sofa—"while I fix us a drink."

All the while he was busy, Leslie speculated about his strange behavior. She also wondered at her own reasons for allowing him to dominate her so completely. It was entirely out of character for her. She'd never allowed any man, even Charles, such liberties. But Cord was different, and that difference had fascinated her right from the beginning.

When he joined her on the sofa and handed her a drink, she accepted it with a murmured, "Thank you," her gaze meeting and locking with his. For a moment Leslie wondered if her eyes were deceiving her. There appeared to be an element of pain intermingled with the anger emanating from his eyes. She lowered her gaze rather hastily and took a sip of her drink.

"I wasn't aware that aging Greeks with fat bank accounts interested you." His voice as cold as ice. "The two of you seemed to be getting along rather well when I arrived."

Leslie's first thought was to tell him, in no uncertain terms, that it was none of his business. But something held her back. "I was there to cover the party and, if possible, interview Paul Papolous. Fortunately, I was able to do both." She took another sip of the cool, tart mixture, watching him over the rim of her glass.

"Funny"—one dark brow arched, his face a picture of derision—"I didn't get that impression from where I was standing. The two of you were chatting away like old friends."

"As a matter of fact we were. He's a very friendly person. I really enjoyed meeting him."

No sooner had the words left her mouth when Cord grabbed her. The drink in her hand slipped to the carpet as she was crushed against his broad chest. His arms closed around her like bands of steel. Leslie knew he was going to kiss her, and she turned her head. His harsh groan penetrated the tension-filled room as his hand clasped the nape of her neck and forced her head back, "Ah, no, sweetheart, I'll not be denied this." His lips covered hers savagely, brooking no resistance.

Leslie struggled to remain impassive to the demanding assault on her senses, but the strange and inexplicable bond that had been forged between them that first moment proved greater than her efforts to resist. Cord's muttered "Don't fight me, Leslie" was her undoing. She parted her lips to his invading tongue like the unfolding of a delicate pink rose.

Cord shifted her pliant body so that she was lying against the soft cushions of the sofa, his long length beside her. His lips trailed down the fragile slimness of her neck to the creamy swell of her breasts. Leslie's fingers threaded themselves in the luxuriant thickness of his hair as his lips evoked a response from her that was swamping her with its intensity.

Leslie was hardly aware of Cord's fingers finding and easing down the zipper at the back of her dress or of his gently sliding the garment off her shoulders. It was only when his hands came in contact with the firm, taut nipples of her breasts that a low moan of protest escaped her. But before she could follow through, Cord silenced her with his lips, this time with a gentleness that removed all thought of withdrawal, as she responded to his caresses with complete abandonment.

Leslie's fingers became impatient with the material of Cord's shirt separating his body from hers. She tugged at it with an almost frenzied effort, the urge to feel his skin against her own uppermost in her mind. Sensing her efforts, Cord eased away from her enough to quickly deal with the remaining buttons and shrugged his arms out of the garment. He dropped it to the floor in a forgotten heap, and pressed his hair-rough chest against the aching fullness of her breasts.

His face took on a look of ultimate triumph as he caught the soft cry of pleasure that came from Leslie's parted lips, still moist from his kisses. Cord framed her face with his hands, the weight of his body pressing her deeper among the cushions. Her face bore the heated glow of desire. Her green eyes dulled with passion.

Another shift of his powerful body had Cord bracing himself on one elbow, his free hand bent on inflicting a form of erotic torture so exquisite that Leslie was helpless to deny him.

Long, square-tipped fingers began a tantalizing ascent of the creamy mound nearest him, circling, cupping, squeezing, and then gently flicking the roseate tip with practiced expertise that reduced Leslie's breathing to shuddering gasps. The trail blazed by his fingers was closely followed, and the process repeated, by his tongue.

Leslie's mind had been completely expunged of all thoughts and reasoning. It was as though she were viewing the sensual awakening of her body through one small opening in an immense wall of blankness. Her body seemed to have become nothing but a huge mass of nerve endings, each one brazenly alert, shamelessly vying for its own share of excitation.

Cord's features were an enigmatical mask. His lips captured and held first one taut nipple, and then the other, the coil of desire ever tightening in Leslie's stomach. Her precarious flight seemed to be taking her closer and closer toward the edge of the precipice.

She brought her hands to the dark head at her breasts and held it there. She was slowly dying from his touch, and even in that near cataclysmic state she wanted more. The need to surrender totally to him, to merge with him body and soul, becoming paramount with each passion-filled moment.

Cord felt the involuntary quiver of her hips and slid his hand down over her silk-clad stomach, his searching caress bringing a moan of inexpressible pleasure to her lips. Leslie murmured incoherently, her hips rising against the pressure of his hand.

A muttered sigh of annoyance sounded deep within Cord's throat at the barrier impeding his progress. He sat up and caught the bodice of Leslie's dress and eased it down over her hips. Leslie instinctively finished the process by pushing the garment with her foot and letting it fall unheeded to the floor.

Then all at once, she was in his arms again, delighting in the touch of his bare skin against her own and feeling as if she could never get close enough to him. With loving hands she kneaded the muscles of his broad shoulders, drawing his full weight to rest on her body, aching for release for the gnawing desire that licked at her limbs like ragged flames on a maddening course.

Suddenly she felt the brush of cool air touch her body. She opened dazed eyes to see Cord standing beside the sofa. His hands were busy with unbuckling the narrow belt at his waist, but it was his expression that caught and held her attention.

There was a trace of grimness etched in the depths of his eyes along with desire. But it was that strange gleam, combined with the purposeful movements of his hands that caused a curious sadness to pervade the numbed recess of Leslie's mind.

Whether from the held-back breath that she slowly expelled or the curious expression of regret that crowded her features Cord's hands stilled at his waist. He turned his head slightly, his gaze slitted as he stared knowingly at her.

He kneeled by the sofa in an unexpected move and buried his face in the curve of her neck, his tongue gently caressing the tiny pulse that throbbed there.

"Please stay with me, Leslie," he whispered against her ear. "I can't get you out of my mind," he groaned. "You're like a drug, and I've become addicted."

Leslie didn't push him away, but Cord sensed her withdrawal from him. His hands dropped to her shoulders and he gave her a slight shake. "Don't freeze up on me, Leslie," he demanded harshly. "You want me just as much as I want you."

"I can't," she whispered, bringing her palms up against his chest. "Please, Cord, I can't." Her eyes were reflections of the agony going on inside her. She wanted him, wanted him with a depth of desire that was numbing. And yet something held her back, kept her from giving in to his demands and the overwhelming demands of her own body. Perhaps it was the fact that to him it was a purely basic need, without any words of love. Nothing but cold, bare sex.

"Please, I'd like my dress." She forced herself to speak calmly, determined not to let him see just how deeply his lovemaking had affected her.

"And if I refuse?" he softly asked, one hand reaching up to push back the tumbled hair from her forehead. "What would you do?" There was a certain wariness in his gaze as he waited for her answer.

"Somehow I don't think you'll do that, Cord. It would only prove humiliating for us both."

He stared at her for what seemed like an eternity, the impenetrable mask she'd seen before slipping into place with resolute swiftness. In an unbroken move he sat up and reached for her dress. He watched as she slipped it over her head and smoothed it back in place. Cord reached behind her and eased the zipper closed.

One hand slid possessively over the silk-clad shape of her breasts, the other tangled itself in her hair. "You do realize that I could make you want to stay, don't you?" he softly asked, the cruel curve of his mouth and the harshness in his face belying the soft tone of his voice.

Leslie turned her face into the back of the sofa to escape his knowing eyes. She knew that what he said was true, but to admit it openly to him was unthinkable.

But Cord wasn't satisfied. He caught her chin in a firm grip and forced her to look at him. "Don't turn away from me, Leslie. I want to hear you admit it," he demanded.

She struggled to hold back the tears that were hovering just beneath the surface, her eyes silently pleading with him for understanding. "Say it!" he whispered harshly, his hands hot on her shoulders.

"All right, damn you! I liked it. I wanted you to make love to me. Now are you satisfied?" she cried, the tears breaking through and easing down her face like tiny pearls of dew.

Cord remained poised over her, seemingly fascinated by the sight of her tears. He leaned down and let the tip of his tongue gently lick the moisture from her face. Leslie fought to remain motionless, but the erotic gesture was sending a shiver of pleasure throughout her body. She turned her head away from him. "Please," she whispered.

He pushed himself upright and moved some distance from her. Leslie drew her legs beneath her and pressed as close to her end of the sofa as she could get. *Oh, God,* she thought, *what have I let myself in for?* She refused to look at him, feeling humilated by her show of weakness, her willingness in their love-making. It was the first time she'd ever let her emotions get so out of hand. Why did it have to be with someone so completely ruthless?

"Why didn't you tell me that you had been married?" Cord's voice, harsh and unyielding, demanded. Leslie looked at him in surprise. It wasn't that she'd intentionally kept her marriage and divorce a secret, but for some reason there had never seemed an appropriate moment to tell him.

"Who told you?"

"George. I went back to the office after lunch, and we spent quite a while talking. In the course of the conversation your name came up. He remarked that you seemed to be bouncing back rather well from your disastrous marriage. I managed to conceal my surprise, and then I pumped him."

"Pumped him?"

"Encouraged him to talk, egged him on, whatever you want to call it," he gestured indifferently with one hand. "I was inordinately interested and it seemed a perfect opportunity to learn more about you. After that, I filched your file from personnel." He made the admission without the slightest hint of embarrassment. But in doing so, it only reinforced her initial belief in his ruthlessness.

"That's horrible," she lashed out angrily. "You didn't have to sneak around and question the people I work with. I'm perfectly capable of telling you anything you want to know."

103

"Are you?" he asked sneeringly.

"Yes. But discussing my private life with strangers has never been a practice of mine," she snapped back. At that point her anger was equal to his own. He'd barged into an important assignment and treated the hostess and guests to an example of his rudeness. He'd subjected her to a savage attack, and now she learned he'd been snooping around, prying into her personal affairs.

"Tell me about him." It was put gently, completely taking Leslie by surprise. The softly spoken tone also silenced the angry retort she was about to hurl his way.

"I can't. It's too personal," she murmured, wary of the abrupt change in his manner.

Cord reached over the length of the sofa and grasped her arms. In one swift move she found herself sitting on his lap. His arms slid around her shoulders and hips as he settled her against him. He pressed her head against his chest and rested his face against the softness of her hair. "I have to know, Leslie. It's been eating away at me like some incurable disease ever since George told me. I'm having a difficult time accepting the fact that another man has made love to you. I could quite easily kill him."

Leslie lifted her head and stared at him, shocked by the vehemence in his voice. "Why? It's past history. Besides, I don't like talking about Charles, so let's drop it."

He crushed her to him, an odd hoarseness detectable in his voice when he spoke. "No, damn you, we will not let it drop," he rasped. "I know he was unfaithful, but how badly did it scar you? Is that the reason for that wistful look that creeps into your eyes when you think no one's watching you?"

She tried to jerk away, but he forcibly held her closer. "Oh, no, I want you close to me. If I can't have your body trembling with passion, I can at least derive some satisfaction from feeling you tremble with anger! Now talk, damn you, or I swear, I'll make love to you here and now."

"I hate you, Cord Langdon. You're nothing but a selfish bastard," she lashed out, twisting and pushing until she was sitting beside him instead of on his lap. He allowed her that small concession, but one arm remained on the back of the sofa behind her shoulders, the other one ready to stop her at the first sign of flight.

She glared mutinously. "I was hurt, but I think I'm over it now. The one thing I did gain from the experience was sense enough not to become involved with anyone remotely resembling Charles."

Cord smiled that sardonic smile, a knowing gleam in his eyes. "Am I to conclude by that irrational statement that you consider me in the same category as your former husband?"

Leslie gave him a chilling look, the urge to slap his face almost overcoming her better judgment. "Yes. You both go through life taking what you want without a thought or care for others." She sat forward on the sofa, looking for her shoes that had become lost in the scuffle.

"Are you looking for these?" Cord asked tauntingly. Leslie turned toward him, only to see her shoes dangling from his hand, an amused grin on his rugged face.

She moved forward and made a grab at his hand. He jerked back, and she sprawled across his lap in an ungainly heap. She felt his hands on her shoulders, turning her over to face him. "Leslie, Leslie," he chided mockingly, shaking his head as he spoke. "There's no reason to throw yourself at me, honey, no reason at all. In fact," he whispered, his dark head coming closer, "you don't even have to ask."

His mouth closed over hers then, his lips and tongue combined in an erotic assault on her that soon had her burning with pure, unadulterated desire. She tried to fight him, hitting out, pushing with all her strength, but it only fanned the flames of passion that threatened to rip them both apart.

Slowly her arms were stilled, and instead of fighting they stole around his naked shoulders. Her nails dug into the muscles of his back as her body was wracked with a fit of trembling.

Cord lifted his head to stare at her warm, flushed face. He traced the outline of her lips with one finger. "You're a very stubborn minx, Leslie Garrison. But this is one battle you're going to lose," he whispered. After touching her lips briefly with his, he lifted her to sit beside him.

Leslie ran her hands over her flushed cheeks and through her tousled hair. She closed her eyes against all that had happened. All her carefully erected rules were in complete shambles. She gave a start as she felt one foot being grasped, and the cool fit of her shoe. She opened her eyes and looked down. Cord was on one knee, fastening the tiny buckle that held her shoe in place. His thick hair was in casual disarray from her wandering fingers. The urge to reach out and smooth it was quickly stifled. Any contact with him was as explosive as some highly flammable fuel. Her gaze moved on to his shoulders, smooth and tanned, and to the perfectly toned muscles. Leslie felt a telltale blush steal over her face as she saw the marks left by her fingernails.

Cord glanced up at that moment and caught her look of embarrassment. He smiled, his strong white teeth in stark contrast with his dark face. He reached up and cupped her face with his palms. "Don't look so stricken, honey. I'll wear these scars with the utmost pleasure. They only reaffirm my original impression of you."

Leslie didn't dare ask what that was, she was too cowardly. She sat quietly while he finished fastening the other shoe. When that was done, he stood and reached for her hands, drawing her up against him. "Will you have lunch with me tomorrow?" he asked, his lips raining light kisses over her face.

She let her head rest against his chest, her body

still weak from her encounter with him. "I can't, I have an appointment," she whispered.

"Cancel it," he ground out through clenched teeth.

"I ca—"

"Either you cancel it or I'll speak with George." He interrupted her.

"All right, I'll take care of it," she replied wearily, ignoring his pleased look at her easy capitulation. She was tired and overwrought, ready to agree to almost anything. In less than three hours, her entire life had been picked up, buffeted about, and scattered, much the same as if a tornado had sucked her into its whirling center. Nothing in her past experiences had prepared her for Cord or his disruptive influence in her life. At the moment all she wanted was to be alone, find some quiet corner in which to calm her bruised emotions.

While Cord dressed, Leslie walked over to the French doors and opened them. She stepped out onto the flagstone terrace and the quietness of the night. The breeze coming in off the canal, while not cold, was pleasant. She walked to the edge of the smooth stones and leaned against the railing, her arms hugging her body protectively. *Well, my girl, you've really opened a can of worms this time,* she reflected wryly.

As her hurt had worn off, she had come to pity Charles for his weakness. The failure of their marriage was as much her fault as his. She'd been in love with the idea of love, not once looking beyond the handsome face to the real man. Had she done so, the flaws in his character would have been plainly visible. Whereas, with Cord, she knew right from the beginning what to expect. Weakness was an unknown quantity in his makeup. She remembered what Paul Papolous had said earlier about taking risks in order to succeed. He had unknowingly described Cord to the letter.

The soft click of the doors sounded behind Leslie. She turned to see Cord, his shirt and jacket once more in place, walking toward her. She clenched her fists in an effort to control the quickening of her pulse as he neared.

He joined her by the railing, his arm brushing against hers as he gripped the rail with his hands. There was an unusual air of thoughtfulness about him as he stared out into the night that caused the skin on Leslie's neck to tingle.

She waited for him to say he was ready to take her home. When he showed no signs of doing so, she reminded him that it was late and she was ready to leave.

Cord turned to face her, his gaze stern and searching. "There's one thing I have to know first. Do you still love him?"

Leslie gave a rough sigh. He was incredible, chipping away until one wanted to scream. She returned his gaze unflinchingly. "His name is Charles Brien, Cord. It won't contaminate you if you say it. As to your question"—she turned to look out over the wide sweep of lawn—"no, there's no love left for him. I'm not sure there ever was. I honestly think I was infatuated with him more than anything. He was five years older than me, handsome, and witty." She gave a low humorless laugh. "I was the envy of all my friends, except for Miriam. She tried to point out some things about him that bothered her, but I wouldn't listen. Unfortunately, her predictions came true."

"Do you see him often?" He persisted in his sharp questioning.

"No. As a matter of fact, I haven't seen him since I left Chicago."

After she answered his questions, Cord seemed satisfied. He took her home but was strangely silent during the drive, not an angry silence as he'd shown earlier, but an unsettling one.

She wasn't so foolish as to disregard the inexplicable bond between them, the air of electricity that filled the room when they were together. And after what had taken place earlier, she had even more to think about.

When they reached her apartment, Leslie turned and gave him a tremulous smile. "Thank you for bringing me home, Cord." It sounded inane and out of place, but, then, the entire evening had taken on a air of unreality.

Ignoring her quiet display of good manners, he got out of the car and came around to help her out.

"Don't worry, Leslie"—his lips twitched suspiciously—"I'm not going to spend the night. I'm simply old-fashioned enough to want to see you to your door," he said quietly. She didn't comment, but a surge of relief flooded over her as she caught the amusement in his voice.

He was as good as his word, and after waiting until she unlocked the door, he leaned down and gently kissed her on the lips. He stepped back and smiled. "Don't forget, we have a date for lunch tomorrow," he reminded her.

"I won't forget," she murmured huskily.

Long after he'd gone and she was in bed, Leslie was still attempting to sort out the events of the evening and her own battered emotions. She could still feel the warmth of his hands on her body as they had sent a shaft of desire through her entire being.

She buried her face in the pillow, embarrassment flooding over her as she remembered her own part in their lovemaking. Perhaps she hadn't willingly forced a showdown between them, but she had certainly participated readily enough. Her cheeks burned at her complete abandonment of restrictions. He'd evoked a desire in her that would have ended with them in bed, if he hadn't been gentleman enough to respect her wishes.

Leslie knew her feelings for him went deeper than she was ready to accept. In the back of her mind she knew she would have to deal with those feelings, and soon. Cord was not a patient man. He'd shown that in his quick pursuit of her. And yet, an affair seemed so cold, so indifferent. Could she settle for such a relationship with him?

She'd learned about love and its disappointments the hard way, and when she loved, she gave her all. It would be impossible for her to enter into an arrangement with Cord and be forced to hold back her emotions. She'd seen friends after such an affair was ended feeling sick and miserable. A deep, ragged sigh escaped her as she forced herself to look at Cord objectively. If he'd been serious about settling down, he couldn't have reached his present age without some woman snapping him up. Any fool could see that he was a made-to-order playboy.

## CHAPTER SEVEN

The next morning at her desk, Leslie wondered if the few hours she'd taken off the day before had been worth it. During that brief time it seemed that the amount of work on her desk had doubled.

While she worked, her thoughts inadvertently turned to Cord and the fact that she would be seeing him in a few hours. In spite of the stern lecture she'd given herself the night before, Leslie found herself eagerly awaiting his appearance.

When Miriam called her in for a rundown on the party given by Lila Ames, Leslie couldn't resist gloating just a little over the fact that her interview with Paul Papolous has gone so well. She watched closely as Miriam went over the rough draft she'd worked up. "Well," she said impatiently, "what do you think of it?"

"I'm impressed," the older woman declared. "And George will be also. You've presented the subject in an unusual and quite human light." She smiled at Leslie as she returned the copy. "I think this is your best piece yet."

"Thank you. But, I must add, the man was an absolute dear. He's such a warm and interesting person. I was really puzzled as to how to go about trying to get an interview, when he singled me out for a cozy little chat."

Miriam chuckled. "I see," she drawled, jumping to the obvious conclusion, wrongly so, of course.

"No, you don't," Leslie quickly corrected. "I think Lila had spoken with him about me earlier. I'm also sure that if he hadn't felt he could trust me to be discreet, he would never have been so open."

"Well, from the looks of your article, I'd say you were quite a hit with him. By the way, did Cord ever reach you last night?"

"Cord?" Leslie asked surprised.

"Yes. He called me shortly after eight o'clock and wanted to know if you were busy. I told him about the Ameses party," Miriam explained.

"So . . ." Leslie murmured. "That's how he knew where I was."

"What do you mean?" Miriam asked, her curiosity getting the best of her.

Leslie shrugged. "He came in while I was talking

114

with Paul Papolous, and he wasn't at all friendly. I didn't think to ask him how he knew I'd be there, I merely assumed he was friends with the Ameses."

"Oh, he is. But I happen to know he doesn't go in for parties very much."

The knowledge that Cord had tracked her down gave Leslie some disturbing moments as the morning wore on. Each time she thought she had him safely labeled and tucked in a neat slot, he would surprise her by acting completely out of character. But then, that didn't really surprise her. Being the active head of his own corporation attested to his keen ability to disarm his competitors and manipulate people. So dealing with one recalcitrant female wouldn't bother him in the least, she thought moodily.

In the weeks that followed, their relationship underwent a slow but definite change. Leslie stopped seeing other men, and as far as she could tell, Cord was not dating other women. And even though she was still somewhat reluctant to believe his motives were anything but ulterior, she was constantly amazed by his unguarded jealousy.

She was no longer surprised when he would suddenly appear at any of the parties or events she covered. He kept abreast of her schedule—knowing where and what she was covering as well as she did. Of course the gossips in the office were having a field day. Leslie soon grew accustomed to walking in on small groups of her co-workers who would immediately stop talking and look guilty. Only Carol and Miriam kept her from blowing her cool.

"Ignore them, Leslie," Carol laughingly told her. "They aren't really that bad, but Cord is rather spectacular. I'm almost envious myself."

Leslie merely smiled. Confiding in anyone about her relationship with Cord was impossible. "He's taking me to lunch, so I'll ask if he has a friend for you," she teased.

"Do that, but make sure he's just as handsome and wealthy as Cord." Carol instructed her in mock seriousness as she left Leslie's office.

Later, when Cord did come to her office, Leslie was aware of his presence even before she saw him. She was talking on the telephone, and had swung her chair around so that she was facing the window. Suddenly the skin on the back of her neck began to tingle. She forced herself to turn slowly, and found him leaning against her desk, the thick carpet having allowed him to move silently.

Leslie completed her conversation in short order and replaced the receiver, aware every minute of his appraising gaze resting on her face. She looked up at him and smiled. "Hello," she said, her voice husky.

Cord sat on the edge of the desk. "Hello, green eyes," he returned warmly. After a quick glance at his watch, he asked, "Are you about ready?"

"Why not?" she replied, suddenly feeling light-hearted and gay. "I don't think I'm likely to get to the bottom of this," she said, indicating the pile of work still to be done, "for hours yet. Perhaps a break will help me concentrate better." She opened a drawer and removed her handbag, and then walked over to tell Miriam that she was going to lunch. As they were leaving the office, Leslie saw Cord's gaze straying toward the framed photograph of her father that was back in place on her desk. She'd broken the frame several weeks ago, and had only that morning picked up a new one.

"Who's that, another of your older admirers?" he asked curtly as he caught her elbow and escorted her down the corridor.

At first she was tempted to let him think the worst. But after having seen several examples of his jealousy, she thought better of it. "His name is John Garrison and he's my father." For once she had the unique privilege of witnessing Cord at a loss for words. He had the grace to look discomfited and gave her a sheepish grin. "No comment?" she teased, enjoying, for once, the upper hand.

He reached out with one hand and let his fingers trail down her cheek. "No comment, other than to say I'm relieved. At least I won't have to wonder about him."

Leslie let the conversation drop, but she was secretly pleased by his statement. This happy frame of mind lasted all during lunch. It was while they were enjoying a leisurely cup of coffee afterward that Cord jolted her out of her rose-colored mood.

"We'll be going to my place after we leave here,"

he informed her with a perfectly straight face. "I asked George if I could borrow you for the afternoon. I didn't bring my secretary along on this trip, and I've got some letters that need to be taken care of." The look he leveled at her across the table was a knowing one. He was sitting back in his chair, and to the casual observer he looked relaxed. But Leslie knew better. He was like a tiger, poised before the attack.

"I'm flattered that you thought of me, but I'm afraid it's out of the question. I've tons of work on my desk, as you know. Besides, there are some excellent typists in the typing pool that can do a much better job than I can."

His expression barely changed as he listened to her. "I'm sure any of the young ladies in question would do a nice job, but I don't want them, I want you." He signaled the waiter for the check and then stood. "Shall we go?" he asked coolly.

*And here we go again!* Leslie silently fumed. She walked ahead of him out of the restaurant, her chin held at a defiant angle. He'd stoop to any level to get his way, regardless of the other person's feelings. She bitterly resented his high-handed ways.

When she reached the car, she quickly opened the door and got in, then slammed it with resounding force. Cord merely smiled at her childish behavior and walked around to the other side. Once seated, he turned to face her. "All right, why are you so angry?"

Leslie turned and glared at him, her green eyes sparkling with indignation. "I resent being handed around like a sack of potatoes. George doesn't have the faintest idea of the amount of work I have to get out. And since he saw fit to give you an office, why didn't he supply a secretary as well?" she angrily replied. "Regardless of how casually you sail through life, there are those of us who have a job and responsibilities." She swung away and sat as far from him as the seat would allow.

"Leslie," Cord spoke softly, "look at me." When she showed no inclination of doing so, he leaned over and caught her chin with his thumb and forefinger, forcing her head round. "I really do have some work that needs to go out. As to using one of the typists"— he smiled—"it never entered my mind. I want to be with you. And after the last few weeks I kind of thought you felt the same way. Am I wrong?"

She fidgeted under his searching gaze, her mind going over a succession of hateful retorts trying to find one suitable enough to hurl at him. But something in his face stopped her—some glimmer of sincerity she'd not seen before. It was almost as though it had surfaced without his knowledge, getting around the unreadable mask that always shielded him so well. She twisted out of his grasp, strangely moved by what she'd seen. "No, you aren't wrong."

"Then why are you fighting me?"

Leslie sighed. "You frighten me. Everything seems

119

to be moving too fast." She shook her head. "It's confusing."

Cord gave a low chuckle as he straightened and then started the engine. "I think," he said in an amused voice, "that one Miss Leslie Garrison is running for her life." He caught her hand which was lying on the seat between them and lifted it, his lips caressing her palm. "You can fight all you want, honey, but I'll win in the end," he gently taunted her.

When they reached his home and Cord had shown her into the library, Leslie was surprised to see that he hadn't been kidding. The surface of the large desk was almost completely covered with folders, charts, and correspondence. He removed a few books from the chair at one end of the desk and waved her toward the now empty seat. "Sit down, honey, while I sort through this."

Leslie sat patiently while he worked, enjoying watching him without having to worry about his catching her in her bold appraisal. She let her eyes feast on his dark hair and the way it struggled against the smooth look he preferred and his face that could radiate such anger one moment and then become so gentle the next. There were so many things about him that were precious to her, things she would lock away in her heart. And when he was gone, she would have a wealth of memories.

Her pleasant interlude was broken by the harsh reality that her thoughts had forced upon her. In her heart she knew Cord would be leaving soon. The past

120

weeks he'd spent in determined pursuit of her would soon bore him, and he would be off to another place and more willing feminine companionship. Leslie was unaware of the ragged sigh that escaped her or the bleak expression that now showed in her eyes. On catching that faint sound, Cord looked up for a moment, his sharp gaze colliding with her regretful one.

"Are you ready for some dictation?" he asked briskly, his lips tightening as he took in the change in her emotions.

"Of course," she answered, hurriedly masking her expression and smiling broadly. *Why worry over the inevitable?* she mentally berated herself. *You've known all along that he isn't the staying kind; he's as elusive as an eagle that soars the great plains.*

After dictating several letters in rapid succession, Cord left her to type them and went off to some other part of the house. Leslie drew a sigh of relief at his departure. It would have been impossible to have typed with his far too knowing gaze boring into her back. She inserted paper into the ancient machine and began typing. The letters were quite technical and required all her concentration. At least it gave her mind a brief respite from the tormenting thoughts that constantly plagued her.

The abrupt opening of the library door caused Leslie to swing round from the large picture window where she was standing, her features still reflecting the mood of pensiveness. Cord stood poised in the opening, one hand braced on the door frame, the other tucked into the waistband of his trousers. He had changed from the suit he'd worn earlier, the white shirt and tie replaced by a light gray sport shirt.

His gaze swept over her then to the letters neatly stacked on the desk and back to her again. He walked into the room. "Why didn't you let me know you were through?" he asked peevishly as he went over and looked at each of the letters.

Leslie smiled at the displeasure in his voice. She was beginning to catch a glimpse of this man's character, and for all his outward appearances of strength and determination, there seemed to lurk an element of uncertainty in his relationship with her.

She joined him as he went over the letters, watching him closely for any sign of error in her work. "I've only been through for a few minutes, Cord," she told him.

He didn't answer her, continuing with his swift examination of her work. Finally he raised his head and smiled at her. "You've done an excellent job, as I thought you would."

She felt strangely pleased at his words of praise. "Who knows, I might decide to change jobs someday."

"Umm," was his only comment as he reached for a pen and scribbled his signature on each letter. "Perhaps you will—change jobs that is—but I doubt you'll become a secretary." He spoke without looking up.

After assuring himself that everything was in order, he straightened and said, "Let's go for a swim."

"But I don't have a suit," she replied, somewhat relieved. Appearing before him in a brief swimsuit was not a soothing thought.

Cord folded his arms across his chest and leaned against the desk, a bright gleam in his dark eyes. "There are several to choose from in one of the guest rooms," he informed her smoothly, watching her struggle for an acceptable excuse. A gentle laugh escaped him as he reached out and caught her by her upper arms and pulled her up against him. His arms slid around her waist. "Do I detect a touch of shyness in the cool, unflappable Miss Garrison?" he teased, his voice muffled in the thickness of her hair.

Those few words of ridicule had the desired effect. Leslie pushed back from his reassuring bulk, annoyance flashing across her face. "Of course not," she hotly denied. "As a matter of fact, a cool swim would be nice." She forced herself to agree.

Cord held her at arm's length, the amusement lurking in his eyes only adding to her embarrassment. "It's the first room on the right," he told her, struggling to control his mirth.

Leslie stared incredulously at the two minuscule pieces of material that made up the brief bikini. Heavens! She certainly wasn't a prude, but it was the skimpiest creation she'd ever seen. She dropped the two pieces on the bed and walked over to the closet to go through the other bathing suits that were hanging there. The styles and sizes ranged from one of ancient vintage, obviously one that had belonged to his Aunt Agatha, to several snazzy numbers, but none that would fit her slender frame.

Well, if she must, she must. She stepped out of her shoes and panty hose and removed her clothes. After donning the white bikini, she stared at her reflection in the mirror, not without a sense of pride in the slim coltish lines of her body and the proud thrust of her breasts.

After selecting a thigh-length terry jacket, Leslie left the room and went to join Cord. As she walked along the hallway she found she wasn't as impressed with the house as she had first imagined. There was a decided lack of warmth about the place. She began to understand Cord's determination to let it go.

When she entered the living room there was no sign of her host. She stood just inside the door, an uncertain frown on her face. After waiting for a moment or two, she decided to go on without him to the pool.

The water looked tempting to Leslie. It held an invitation that was irresistible. She lowered herself into the shimmering softness, amazed at the warmth, and immediately gave over to the pleasure of floating. Her hair fanned out above her head like an undulating cloud. She forced herself to relax and gave in to the pleasure of the moment.

Suddenly the water bucked and heaved as if a tidal wave had disturbed the gentle calmness. At almost the same instant, Leslie felt two hands grip her about her waist. She struggled to free herself but was pulled beneath the surface of the water.

The hold on her loosened and she shot up like a cork. She flung back her head to free her face of the clinging curtain of hair that blinded her. "That was a nasty trick," she spluttered as she struggled to regain her balance.

Cord grinned rakishly at her, his gaze resting on the skimpy bra that hardly covered her creamy breasts. "You were drifting away from me and I didn't like it," came his frank admittance. "I want all your attention."

Leslie didn't have a ready response, so she escaped the strangeness of the moment by slicing neatly beneath the surface of the water in a clean dive. Cord quickly followed suit and joined her in a game of playful nonsense that lasted until they were both winded.

While they were catching their breaths, Leslie's eyes wandered over the tanned, muscled breadth of Cord's shoulders and his hair-rough chest. When she became aware that he was remaining perfectly still, she raised her gaze to meet his shyly. Cord moved toward her with ease in the water, his eyes narrowing as if reading her thoughts.

Leslie turned to evade his outstretched arms, but was brought up short when one of his hands tangled itself in the streaming strands of her hair. She twisted about, the movement bringing a shooting pain to her head as his hold tightened. "You're hurting me," she cried from between clenched teeth.

"Then don't fight me," he warned her.

He transferred his hold to her waist and pulled her hips against his. One hand slid with slow deliberation up her spine to the back of her head. Leslie could feel the water closing over them at the same time as Cord's mouth covered hers.

The impact of the kiss was as devastating as she knew it would be. For a moment she resisted, but her resistance seemed only to incense him. He ground his lips against hers with savage force. When she yielded, it was with an abandonment that rocked them both. Her legs tangled with his, useless as any means of support.

Cord easily brought them back up to the surface of the water. The sudden movement and the abrupt glare of the sun made Leslie react as though she were being rudely awakened from an extremely pleasant dream. She knew she should pull away, but the flame of desire that flared to life within her was unlike anything she had ever known. In the heat of the embrace, her arms found their way around his neck; her breasts were tightly pinned against his chest. Only the thin material of the skimpy top was between them.

She rested her head against the side of his neck, loathe to face the mockery in his burning gaze. Leslie was painfully aware of his hands as they moved over her body in soft gentle caresses. It was as if he knew what she was experiencing and was determined not to let the moment end.

When his hands stopped their seeking and paused at the back fastening of the brief bikini top, Leslie murmured protestingly.

"Shhh . . ." Cord silenced her, his lips taking over where his quiet rebuke ended. As with all the other times before, his wish became the dominating force. Leslie felt rather than saw him fling the bikini top toward the chaise longue where her beach jacket was laying.

Nipples taut and rigid met with a bronzed chest, the crisp mat of hair causing a rough, slightly abrasive sensation, causing Leslie to break away from the stirring pull of Cord's lips and, instead, bite the skin of one broad shoulder.

There was a grunt of surprise from Cord. He pulled back and looked down at Leslie, a triumphant gleam in his dark eyes. "How much longer, Leslie?" He brought his hands round and cupped her breasts. His gaze dropped, seemingly fascinated by his power over her body.

Suddenly the craziness of the situation penetrated her senses. Leslie twisted out of Cord's arms with a quick, unexpected move. She swam to the ladder and climbed out of the pool. He watched her as she reached for the white scrap of material and hurriedly cover herself. With hands not quite steady, she picked up a towel and began to rub the excess water from her hair. After a moment Cord followed her.

The towel was taken from her hands and she was forced to meet his burning gaze. "Why did you bolt, Leslie? What are you afraid of ?" There was a tenseness about him that was different. She was accustomed by now to his anger and mockery, but this was something new.

She dropped her eyes, unable to withstand the harsh penetrating stare. "I was cold. It's starting to get dark," she murmured evasively. She bent to retrieve the terry jacket, but Cord snatched it from her hand. "I don't want you to cover yourself, damn it! It's just one less layer I'll be forced to peel away in order to get to the real you."

He reached for a cushion from one of the chairs and dropped it on the concrete close beside him. "Sit down! I'll rub your hair dry," he told her in a gruff voice.

The feel of his large hands on her hair was remarkably relaxing to Leslie. At a slight pressure from his arm on her shoulder she allowed her body to rest against him. His thighs were on either side of her and her face brushed that hair-rough part of his body as he gently rubbed her hair. "Have dinner with me tonight," he murmured.

"All right," she replied in a whisper, giving in to the exquisite feeling of lethargy that was slowly spreading over her body. Cord stopped using the towel, and his hands began kneading the tense muscles in her neck and shoulders. Her head lolled about as though she had no control over it, while she gave in to the thrilling touch of his hands on her body.

"When are you going to stop fighting me, Leslie?" he asked. The question was put gently, but the subject left her with a feeling of panic. She knew she was only prolonging the inevitable, but her pride wouldn't let her give in without a struggle. "Are you still comparing me to Charles?" Cord asked.

Leslie moved forward out of reach of the hands that had afforded her so much pleasure. She spread one of the large towels on the concrete and stretched out on her stomach. She knew Cord was waiting for an answer, but she wanted to avoid it as long as possible.

After what seemed like an eternity, Leslie rested the upper portion of her body on her elbows as she considered his question. She'd hoped he would let the subject drop, but from the strained silence and his eyes boring into her back, she realized the futility of such a wish. "No, not any longer. You're not like Charles in the least, Cord. He's weak, and you're not. But that strength you possess can be just as frightening," she admitted.

"That's a cop-out, Leslie, and you know it. It's not me you're afraid of, it's yourself. You've subjugated your emotions for so long, you're shocked and embarrassed to find that you are capable of white, hot passion, strong enough to make you want to forget all the little rules you've planned your life by," he ruthlessly pointed out.

She sat up and wrapped her arms around her drawn-up legs and rested her chin on her knees. She allowed her hair to swing between them like a curtain against his penetrating stare. "You make me sound like some cold, calculating female," she replied huskily. "I've always had rules, as you call them, that I've lived by. But, then, doesn't everyone? The only difference is that now I'm more cautious than before. One of those rules was that when I married it would be forever."

Cord waved aside her explanation with careless disregard. "I can't buy that. While I'm sorry you were hurt, I would like to point out that divorce isn't the worst thing that could have happened to you. You're young and beautiful, with a promising career. There's plenty of women who aren't so fortunate."

Leslie turned and stared at him, anger flashing in her green eyes. "Why do you have to put everything in such cold, stark terms?" she lashed out. "I was the one hurt, not you! I had to make the decision to leave, admit defeat."

"You might have left him physically, but emotionally you're still tied to him," Cord snapped in a steely voice.

"Why can't you just forget it?" she cried. "For a while today I thought we were beginning to understand each other, but you refuse to leave my past alone."

"There's a simple enough explanation for that," he calmly replied, ignoring her outburst. "You can't forget it. You compare each man you meet with him, withdrawing more and more into the shell that has become your refuge."

"Is there some crime against protecting myself against things that hurt?"

"Not at all, but it does become a crime when you allow it to rule your life. Every man isn't like Charles, Leslie, and you were made to be loved by a man. Each time I've held you in my arms you've struggled like a wildcat. But when I refused to let you go, you responded like the warm person you are."

"So?" she asked in a short voice.

"So I'm determined that you stop retreating. I know you have a love-hate feeling for me that's gnawing at you. That's better than no feelings at all, and I'm very determined."

"You are also very cruel," she whispered.

"I don't deny that, but for some reason you make me want to hurt you," he confessed. "I hate the thought of your having ever belonged to another man!"

The confession was uttered with a forcefulness that surprised Leslie. Why should he care? He made it sound like she had committed a crime. "I suppose you have a lily-white past?" She posed the question on a derisive note.

Cord ignored the question. Leslie looked at him, surprised by his silence. He was staring at her through half-closed lids, a brooding tautness etched on his rough features. "I want you, Leslie."

His powerful body was stretched along the length of the chaise beside her. She allowed her eyes to take in his every inch, hating him for forcing her to remember the hateful details that had once been a part of her life. Hating him for his persistent chipping away at her carefully erected facade. Only a man as incredibly pushy as he was would continue the unpleasant inquisition. She closed her eyes. "I'm sorry, Cord, but I can't."

He reached down and gathered her up in his arms and swung her onto his lap. Leslie was so surprised by his sudden move, she could only stare at him in astonishment. "You will learn that I'm not a man to be put off by petty excuses, Leslie, nor am I known to be a quitter."

"You should also add brutal to that list, Cord," she snapped. "You dismiss all thoughts and feelings that aren't of your own making as being ridiculous. Well, I didn't ask for your opinions, so keep them to yourself." She came to her feet in one quick move and reached for the terry jacket. She turned and glared at him. "And while we're on the subject, please leave me alone. I'm tired of your incessant criticisms," she declared frostily, and stalked off.

All the while she dressed Leslie muttered and thrashed about angrily. The small glimpse of understanding that had surfaced at lunch had been swept away by Cord's brutal words, their cut as abrasive as a piece of rough sandpaper, leaving her raw and bleeding.

She jerked the blue linen skirt into place and fastened it, and then hurried over to the old-fashioned dresser to comb her tangled hair. She forced the comb through the snares and tangles with a force that brought tears to her eyes. She hated him! He was the rudest, most inconsiderate brute she'd ever met. The sooner he finished his business in Miami and left, the happier she'd be. After adding a touch of makeup and light lipstick, Leslie picked up her purse and left the room.

When she stepped into the hall, the door opposite the bedroom she'd been using opened. Cord, now dressed in a dark blazer and light trousers, let his gaze run over Leslie before speaking. "We'll stop at your place first so that you can change," he spoke determinedly, ignoring the fire shooting from her eyes.

"I'm sorry, but I've changed my mind. I can't have dinner with you." She spoke coolly. Nothing on earth could induce her to spend one more evening in his detestable presence.

"In that case we'll eat at your place," he countered smoothly, moving toward her with pantherlike ease. Leslie stared incredulously. Damn him! He knew she found that idea just as unacceptable.

She steeled herself for his touch on her arm, hating the traitorous feeling of desire that sprang up. Even in anger he had the power to speed her appetite to a gnawing hunger for the feel of his hands on her body. She allowed him to steer her down the hall and out the front door to the car. As he held open the door to the car and waited for her to get in, he asked, "What's it to be?"

Leslie smoothed her skirt unnecessarily and held her purse on her lap like some aging spinster about to take her weekly drive. She ran the tip of her pink tongue over her bottom lip nervously. "We'll go out," she murmured, never taking her eyes off the large tree directly in front of the car.

Cord laughed, one large hand reaching in to cup the back of her neck for a brief moment. "Coward," he whispered mockingly. In seconds he'd withdrawn his hand and was striding around the front of the car.

In the course of the drive Cord asked Leslie several questions about her father. Leslie, at first tongue-tied by anger, jumped at the chance to talk about something other than her personal life. She had no difficulty presenting her father in a favorable light. Cord glanced at her several times as she talked, his sharp gaze taking in the love in her face and voice as she spoke.

"The two of you seem very close," he said.

Leslie nodded. "We are. And yet we each lead our separate lives. Right now he's going through a bad stretch with Monica, my stepmother. It seems fairly certain to end in a divorce."

Cord looked surprised for a moment. "Have they been married long?"

"Several years. After my mother died, Monica lost

134

no time in securing her position. I'm surprised that it's lasted as long as it has."

The conversation drifted from one thing to another for the rest of the way, and Leslie, in spite of her earlier resolve to ignore him, found herself enjoying the easy moments they were sharing. It was really incredible, she mused, how their relationship vacillated from anger one moment to complete enjoyment of each other the next.

Cord brought the car to a stop in front of Leslie's apartment building and switched off the engine. He turned toward her, one arm snaking out to rest behind her head. "Is it safe for me to wait inside, or are you still angry?" he asked in that blandly innocent voice that she was beginning to recognize so well. Even though she knew he was silently laughing at her, it pricked at her conscience.

He'd brought out into the open blunt truths that Leslie had not wanted to face, much less listen to. Her reaction had stemmed from a combination of guilt and embarrassment. "Nonsense," she answered calmly, avoiding his gaze. "You're welcome to your opinions, Cord." She reached for the handle and opened the door, and then said sweetly, "You've admitted that you enjoy hurting me, so I simply attributed your petty attack to the fits of paranoia you seem to suffer from." She stepped from the car and slammed the door.

Cord got of the car and was beside her almost before she could blink an eye. "Paranoid am I?" he demanded grimly, taking her by the elbow and rushing her inside. Leslie glanced up toward his face at the threatening tone of his voice, the taut muscles of his face leaving her even less assured. When they reached her apartment, she groped in her purse for the key, but Cord took it from her fumbling fingers before she could use it.

He flung open the door and pushed Leslie into the room and slammed the door closed. "Now"—he spoke in a barely controlled voice, his hold on her arms tightening—"explain that last remark." There was such a blazing anger emanating from his eyes, Leslie could almost feel the heat.

Her chin rose as she stubbornly stood her ground. Her green eyes were bright with emotion. "What's the matter, Cord? Can't you take criticism? But that's the way it usually is, isn't it? You're quick to point out the error of my ways, painting me as some emotionally frozen nut, but when I take a swipe at you, that's a no-no."

They glared at each other like two antagonists, each fighting to control the urge to lash out. Cord's face was frozen in a mask of disapproval and anger. Leslie's cheeks bore two tiny circles of pink, and her breathing was harsh and ragged.

He was the first to move. He ran one large hand around the back of his neck before turning and walking over to stare out the window. Leslie felt herself relax a fraction, her breathing slowly returning to normal.

She walked over and dropped her purse onto the sofa and then said, "I'll only be a few minutes. Why don't you fix yourself a drink?"

Cord turned, his dark enigmatic gaze revealing nothing. "Take all the time you need, I'll use the time to make a couple of telephone calls." He removed his jacket and draped it across a chair near him.

"Cord," Leslie burst out unexpectedly. "I'm sorry." She turned on her heel and rushed from the room.

Later, as she stood beneath the warm shower, she was still wondering at the reasoning behind her spontaneous apology. She'd had every right to defend herself from his harsh attack but, she rebuked herself, her retaliation had been one of vindictiveness because what he'd said was true. She had buried her emotions since divorcing Charles, refusing to allow anything or anyone to penetrate the protective covering. When Cord shattered the security of that covering, she had panicked, lashing out with all her might.

## CHAPTER EIGHT

Leslie was somewhat taken aback when she entered her bedroom. Cord was stretched out on her bed, talking on the phone. She could see that he'd removed his shoes and his entire pose was one of relaxation.

He turned and looked at her framed in the doorway, one hand clutching the robe tightly around her body. She released her grip to tighten the belt, and then grabbed at the revealing neckline.

Cord abruptly ended his conversation at that point and sat up, swinging his feet to the floor, his hands braced on either side of his body. The lamp on the bedside table cast a soft glow over the harsh plane of his strong features. Leslie took a tentative step forward, wary of his disturbing presence in the close confines of her bedroom.

His eyes were watching her with all the intentness of an eagle about to swoop and grab its prey. She drew a deep, shaky breath and forced herself to calmly walk toward the chest of drawers that stood close to the bed. She'd simply collect her clothes and dress in the bathroom.

When she drew even with Cord, he reached out and caught her by her wrist, stopping her as if she'd suddenly become paralyzed. "You're very beautiful, Leslie," he whispered, his hypnotic gaze holding her mercilessly with its intensity. Leslie forced back the leaping flame of desire that was consuming her and made a half-hearted attempt at pulling her hand from his grasp. With one quick flick of his wrist Cord jerked her down beside him on the bed.

"To hell with dinner," he muttered, shifting his body so that Leslie was lying beneath him. She had only a moment before his mouth covered hers, and in that split second the strange glitter in his eyes was unreadable. All else was lost as the demanding insistence of his kiss began to force a response from her that was quickly turning into an insatiable hunger. His mouth left hers and slipped to her neck. She could feel the tension of his hard body as he pressed against her.

Cord drew a deep, shuddering breath. His face was buried in the creamy softness of her face and neck. "God! Leslie, you are slowly driving me crazy," he

139

whispered. He lifted his head to stare down at her face that desire had softened. One large hand slid up and fitted itself to the curve of one cheek. He kissed her lips with a gentleness that was only barely held in check.

Leslie brought her arms up and around his neck when he would have pulled away. She didn't understand nor was she capable, at the moment, of any sort of clear thinking. He evoked such a feeling of sexual desire, such a need of fulfillment, that all else was blotted from her thoughts.

At her unconscious capitulation Cord's ability to control his need for her was dashed like a piece of fine crystal falling to a stone floor. He had to have her, possess her. She was in his blood like an addiction to some strangely potent drug.

When his hand loosened the robe and slipped it off her shoulders and touched the throbbing fullness of her breasts, Leslie gave a gasp of unrestrained pleasure. She moaned softly as his thumb gently flicked the rigid peaks of her nipples. She insinuated one hand inside the front of his shirt and ran her fingers through the dark hair that covered his chest. In her haste, the buttons of his shirt became undone, and soon her face was pressing against his warm skin, the wild pounding of his heart sounding in her ear.

"Am I dreaming?" he whispered, his tongue leaving a trail of fire from her lips to the rounded softness that was now visible to him. "Beautiful," he muttered, pushing the last of the robe from Leslie's body.

Leslie was incapable of thought. There was only one driving force within her at the moment—her need for Cord and the fulfillment of their desire for each other. He levered himself up on one elbow and reached over and switched off the lamp, casting the room in total darkness. When he reached for Leslie, she met his embrace eagerly.

She was throbbing with an inexplicable urge that glazed her eyes and left her mouth dry. When she tried to speak, Cord stopped her with his lips. Leslie's head fell back, her mouth opening to his and the intimate pressure of his tongue. It darted in and out, tasting the warm sweetness that was offered.

Leslie was vaguely aware of him removing his clothes, but his movements were so deft and smooth that it seemed almost dreamlike. He was unhurried in his lovemaking, his strong sure hands stroking her body, almost making her shriek with the pure joy of it all.

"Touch me, sweetheart," Cord whispered into her ear, the lobe of which he was teasing with his lips. "I want to feel your hands on my body."

At first Leslie refused this terribly intimate request. But matters were taken out of her hands when Cord caught one of her hands and placed it against the warm skin of his thigh. With hesitant, almost jerky movements, she began to work her way over the smooth skin.

Her quest to know better the hidden secrets of the body that had brought so much pleasure to her own added a boldness to her seeking. Suddenly her initial shyness evaporated, and in its stead grew an insatiable curiosity.

It was her turn to be the aggressor and she began to find pleasure in bringing gasps of satisfaction from Cord by touching him. In her newfound headiness, Leslie rose to her knees beside him, caressing the breadth of his shoulders and on down to his chest.

For a moment she concentrated on the responsive peaks of his small nipples nestled in the thick growth of hair. She eased her head down and with her tongue teased and kissed the entire breadth of his chest. The taste of his skin was clean and fresh, lingering pleasantly in her nostrils as she drew back and let her hands continue their exciting journey over his flat stomach and narrow-hipped leanness.

In her mind was the recurring thought of how beautiful he was, how beautifully made. His body, his form, the hollows and planes, reminded her of a fine piece of sculpture, lovingly shaped and created by a master. The full impact of his beauty took her breath away, this rare and exquisite man whom she loved.

Cord, suddenly aware of the stillness of her hands, sighed.

"God! Leslie. Don't stop," he entreated her hoarsely and then raised his head to look at her. "Leslie?" There was a note of tender concern in his voice. Had he pushed her too far? Demanded more than she could give?

Leslie turned toward his dark shape, her breasts brushing against his cheek. "I'm all right, Cord," she murmured as she melted into his arms. "But please . . . please love me."

She was no longer concerned with repercussions—what might be or hadn't been. The woman in her had been awakened by Cord's touch, by the burgeoning love she felt for him and, as such, demanded complete fulfillment.

His caresses carried her to such a peak of awareness that she was twisting and softly whimpering from the fire that leaped within her. She could feel the naked brush of his body on hers, exciting her even further. Her only sane or coherent thought was the intense sense of satisfaction Cord seemed to derive from the feel of his hands on her satin-smooth skin. When the two merged, they were lost as individuals, swiftly thrust toward the euphoric heights of a timeless moment that transcends all normal thought or deed.

When Leslie first began to awaken, she was vaguely aware of a feeling of well-being. She stretched her slim body and luxuriated in the feeling of contentment that surrounded her body and mind. The feel of the sheet as it touched her bare skin was particularly sensual. She turned on her side and snuggled down into the cozy warmth of the bed.

Her eyes swept past and then returned with a rude awakening to the note attached to the pillow next to hers. For a moment she was completely still as the events of the night rushed over her with cold clarity. Cord! Here in her bedroom! He had spent the greater part of the night, and she had been just as eager for him to stay as he had.

Oh, God! She came to a sitting position in a flash and drew her knees to her chest. She looked at the note with misgiving, longing to know what it said but at the same time dreading what she would find. She reached out with a trembling hand and plucked it from the pillow. She read the few boldly scrawled lines, her lips unconsciously curving into a smile. Even his handwriting bore out the strength and determination of his indomitable character. He was needed in Houston and would be back as soon as possible. Nothing flowery, just simple and to the point.

Leslie folded the paper and dropped it onto the table beside her bed. Relief registered on her face for a moment at the realization that she wouldn't be forced to deal with him so quickly after their night of lovemaking. But there was also disappointment that he was gone. She suddenly felt as bereft as a boat loosened from its moorings.

Cord as a lover was so different from the hard and unyielding individual that he seemed. He had been gentle and unhurried, restraining himself until he was certain she was at the same height of ecstasy as he. And afterward he had held her cradled against his chest, whispering endearments that were so tender at that special moment.

Her prior intimate experience had been only with Charles, but there was no comparison. Cord radiated more sensuality from one little finger than Charles did as an entire person.

The time she and Cord spent together had been wonderful, but common sense dictated that she view that time objectively. She knew her pride would never allow her to assume that one night of unbelievable beauty would bind him to her. And yet a continuation of such a relationship wasn't what she wanted. It would leave her even more torn up at its conclusion than her divorce. For whether she wanted to admit it or not, her feelings for Cord had become a vital part of her existence.

Leslie hadn't planned on allowing her relationship with Cord to get so out of hand. But deep down she knew that she had been wanting him to make love to her from the moment she'd encountered that enigmatic gaze of his staring at her from the opened doorway of his aunt's home. Such an admission did little to her waning self-esteem. After chasing the problem around for what seemed like an interminable time with no clear solution in mind, Leslie got out of bed.

Since it was the weekend and there was nothing scheduled for her to cover, it seemed like an excellent time to visit her dad. It would also give her a chance to get away from Cord's disturbing influence. Even though he was away at the moment, everything she touched or saw reminded her of him.

After a quick shower Leslie wrapped a large towel around her body and padded over to the telephone. She dialed Miriam's number, but got a busy signal. She went back to the bedroom and dressed, and then got out a small suitcase and began to pack. When that job was finished, she tried Miriam's number again. "Damn," she muttered at the annoying sound. *Oh, well,* she thought resignedly, *I'll call later.*

After taking her suitcase to the door, she went back to make sure that the coffeemaker had been unplugged and checked the other small items, which had become a habit of long standing. Satisfied that she hadn't forgotten anything, she walked through to the living room. When she passed the telephone, she chewed at her bottom lip in indecision. What if Cord called during the weekend? *Don't be such a ninny,* a little voice mocked her, *you probably won't hear from him for several days.*

Leslie felt like giving in to the tears that had been welling just beneath the surface ever since she had awakened and found Cord gone. But her pride and her innate quest for survival came to her rescue. So what if she had been the super klutz of the year? It had been something very special, and a night she would remember forever.

The drive to Ft. Lauderdale where her dad lived wasn't long, so Leslie drove at a leisurely speed. She was a trifle bit conscience-stricken that it had been so long between visits. But Monica's presence had brought about a dramatic change in the atmosphere of the comfortable sprawling home that Leslie had grown up in.

Approximately a year after her mother's death her father had married Monica Tate. The large gap in the ages, while not unheard of, did cause close friends to look with skepticism upon the union.

Of course Monica was immune to the raised eyebrows and whispers that surrounded her marriage. She was a fighter and let nothing stand in her way of snaring a rich older husband. Her relationship with Leslie, while not openly hostile, was definitely lacking in warmth. For some unknown reason she resented her stepdaughter bitterly.

Fortunately Leslie had been at an age when college was the next phase of her young life, so there had never been an actual confrontation between the two women. But by the air of suppressed irritation and Monica's short manner, Leslie was left in no doubt as to her true feelings.

John Garrison was soon forced to accept the fact that his bank balance was far more attractive to his new wife than he was. Consequently he spent more hours in his office than usual and more time at his club than at home. The bright spot of his life was Leslie.

She was the image of her mother, and John never tired of seeing her. But Leslie had, over the years, forced herself to stay away for longer and longer periods of time. Occasionally John would drive to Coral Gables and take his daughter out to lunch or dinner. It was enjoyable for them both, but not a practice Leslie encouraged because of Monica. Her father's peace of mind was too precious to her, and she knew her stepmother was always especially difficult after each of their outings.

Now, from the tone of his letter, Leslie gathered that all was not well with Monica's little setup. She could only guess at the subtle hints that had been dropped in the few lines she'd received from her father, but she truly hoped that the blinkers had been lifted from his eyes at last.

The excellent speed that had been maintained on the Interstate was brought to an abrupt halt as Leslie crawled along at a snail's pace through the city. Each time she made the trip she was reminded of why some of the residents preferred to do much of their inner-city travel by water. With three hundred miles of canals and pathways for the numerous pleasure craft, it was decidedly more interesting.

Finally, after what seemed like an interminable wait and several muttered expletives, Leslie found herself on the wide, quiet street that had been her home for the first years of her life. The houses sat back from the street in unobtrusive elegance. It was a neighborhood of quiet dignity, where the occupants frowned on ostentatious displays of wealth. Yet, for all the grandeur of the homes, Leslie could remember the warmth of the neighbors, most of whom she had known very well.

As she turned into the long, curving driveway that led to her home, she was struck again by the attractive setting. The house was constructed of stone and cedar siding. There were endless windows, providing an abundance of light. Several tall palms stood in the foreground, surrounded by a velvet carpet of grass. At each end of the house grew a majestic oak, its limbs low and spreading. There were a number of neatly pruned shrubs on either side of the front entrance, bordered by the brilliant burst of red and green caladiums.

She drove on around back, her eyes taking in the cool, shaded patio and the large swimming pool. Here the grounds were one continuous mass of color. All sorts of plants bloomed in profusion. There were also several redwood tubs placed around the pool, waiting to be filled with plants from the greenhouse that was situated in a far corner of the back lawn.

As soon as Leslie brought her car to a stop and opened the door, she could hear the excited barking of MacGregor, the twelve-year-old Scottish terrier. She smiled as he maneuvered his short stocky body between the draperies and the sliding glass door. His frenzied barking was now accompanied by frantic scratching at the barrier of glass separating him from his favorite person.

Leslie chuckled as she got out of the car and reached in the back for her purse and suitcase. Just as she turned, the small missile of hair hurled itself against her body with all the force his age would allow. In that split second Leslie dropped both purse and suitcase in order to catch the excited bundle. She was immediately subjected to a series of licks, interspersed with sharp yelps of joy.

"He hasn't exerted that much energy since your last visit," said John Garrison, as he watched the girl and the dog, a pleased smile on his still handsome face. He closed the gap between himself and Leslie and hugged her, dog and all. MagGregor growled at the flagrant disregard of his presence, glaring menacingly at John. "All right, you old reprobate, she'll be gone in a couple of days, and then where will you be?" he asked laughingly, ruffling the spiky coat of the dog.

Leslie allowed the terrier to slide to the ground and then slipped an arm around her father's waist. She reached up and kissed his smooth cheek. "How are you, Dad?"

His arm around her shoulders tightened perceptibly. "Much better, now that you're here," he confessed huskily. He bent down and retrieved the suitcase and purse, handing the latter to Leslie.

She controlled her facial features at the sign of weariness in his voice and face. "And Monica?" she asked.

"She left several days ago," he replied in somewhat relieved tones. "The divorce will, hopefully, be handled quickly and satisfactorily for us both I think." He took Leslie's elbow and the two of them walked toward the house. "I'm not pining away, so wipe that concerned look off your face, brat," John spoke reassuringly. "We both know this is something that should have been done years ago." He reached for the handle of the sliding door, only to have it slip from his grasp and the door slide open as Nellie Temes appeared in the aperture.

The housekeeper opened her arms to Leslie and hugged the slim body close to the ramrod straightness of her own. She pulled back and held Leslie at arm's length, going over her with her razor-sharp gaze. "You've changed," she stated bluntly. "Still too thin, but your color is better."

Leslie cast a quick grin at her father, who was standing by during Nellie's brief assessment. He gave the housekeeper a wry glance and asked, "Now, may we go inside and not try to cool the entire city of Ft. Lauderdale?"

"Hmmph!" snorted the spry middle-aged woman with a complete disregard for propriety. She pulled Leslie forward into the room and shot an acid look toward John. "Take her suitcase to her bedroom while I fix some sandwiches for lunch," she ordered him. "Now," she informed Leslie, "you can help me and we'll have a nice little chat," she explained as they made their way through the large comfortable den and into the kitchen.

This seemingly innocent remark brought a twinkle to Leslie's eyes. She'd learned at an early age that any time Nellie invited someone to her kitchen for a chat, it was either to impart some choice gossip or pump her unassuming guest for information. Perhaps this time it was Monica who had aroused her curiosity. "How's Dad really taking this divorce, Nellie?" she asked, deciding to do her own snooping first for a change.

Nellie was bustling about, removing several clear-plastic-wrapped dishes from the refrigerator. She cocked her head, stopping for a moment before answering. "How does he appear to you?" she asked, her hands performing the task before her without thought.

Leslie sat on the corner of the butcher-block table, swinging one shapely leg as she considered the question. "He seemed almost relieved, but it could have been wishful thinking on my part."

"I don't think so," the older woman replied. "I've watched him through this whole thing, and I'm convinced that he's quite pleased to be getting out of a situation that's been wrong from the beginning." She went on to tell Leslie that Monica had already latched on to a wealthy Brazilian.

## CHAPTER NINE

Lunch was quickly disposed of, with Nellie resorting to her usual grumbling that neither John nor Leslie were eating enough. They endured her fussing, with each bolting from the room while she busied herself in the kitchen.

Her dad gave Leslie a conspiratorial grin. "Meet me at the greenhouse," he muttered in a low voice as he passed her on his way out. "Even that old harridan won't bother us there."

Leslie laughingly agreed and then hurried to her room to change into something more practical for gardening than the white slacks and silk shirt she was wearing.

As she entered the room that had been hers since infancy, a soft smile curved her lips. She paused a moment before closing the door, her gaze tenderly touching on the different phases of her life so visible before her. Several of her dolls, their outfits only slightly the worse for wear, were still in place on the floor-to-ceiling shelves that took up part of one wall. There was the shell collection that she'd so painstakingly collected one summer, her books—even the bedraggled teddy bear that had been her bed partner for so many years.

She gently closed the door and walked over to the table beside the bed. A framed photograph of her mother stared back at her, her lovely face serene and calm, unaware of the early death that would rob her husband and young daughter of her beloved presence. Leslie rested one hand on the frame for a moment and then moved over to the bed where her bag waited.

As she unpacked the few items of clothing she'd brought with her, it suddenly hit her how the entire atmosphere of the place had changed with Monica's leaving. Gone was the air of conflict, the hint of suppressed anger that lurked behind a smiling veneer that grated so on one's nerves. For the first time in a number of years, Leslie felt comfortable and at ease.

After putting away her clothes, Leslie pushed aside several garments hanging in the closet in order to get to a row of drawers built into the wall. She opened the bottom one and removed an old pair of faded jeans and an equally ancient cotton T-shirt.

She backed out of the closet, her find clutched to her chest. Apparently Nellie had thought them well hidden, but Leslie was accustomed to her little tricks and lost no time in locating her old favorites.

In minutes she was dressed in the jeans and shirt, her long hair drawn back and tied with a white scarf she'd found in a dresser drawer.

It was while she was adding a touch of gloss to her lips that she gave in to her thoughts of Cord. His face was indelibly printed in her mind, and no amount of pretending could erase his image. She replaced the cap on the tube of gloss and then touched her lips with soft fingertips, remembering the feel of Cord's mouth, his lips drawing a response from her that was devastating.

The hours she'd spent in his arms had changed her, and yet they had also exposed her vulnerability. "And all for what?" she whispered. His life-style was an open book for all to see. From the very start he'd made not the slightest effort to conceal the fact that he wanted her. With special emphasis on the word *wanted*. Deep down she knew his open and direct manner had been part of what had drawn her to him. Now she found herself in the sort of situation she'd wanted to avoid—in love with a man who had no intention of committing himself to any type of relationship other than a casual affair. And that, she grimly reminded herself, is that!

Knowing Cord as she did, Leslie had no doubts of

his conducting the affair, if it indeed became one, with the utmost discretion and, likewise, the ending.

She sighed as she walked to the door. All the thinking in the world wouldn't solve the problem, and she was determined not to let her personal problems ruin the weekend.

As she passed through the breakfast room she met Nellie, just emerging from the kitchen. "Honestly, Leslie," the latter scolded. "Why do you insist on wearing such horrible-looking clothes?" She stood poised, her hands on her hips, disapproval clearly written on her homely face.

"Now, Nellie, don't fuss. I'm going to help Dad in the greenhouse and I hardly think the clothes I was wearing suitable for grubbing in potting soil." She pointed this out with quiet patience. A disgusted "hmmph" was the only response offered as Leslie stepped around the older woman and continued on her way.

She found her dad busy transferring several flats of blooming plants from the greenhouse to poolside, ready to transplant them to the large redwood planters.

"What can I do to help, Dad?" she asked. She was anxious to keep busy so that she wouldn't dwell on Cord.

John squatted down and set the flat he was carrying near one of the tubs. "You can start with this one, honey. I think that tub will hold all these plants. If not, you can put the rest in that bed by the fence," he said, nodding toward the sandstone structure that separated his property from his neighbor. He left Leslie on her own and went back to the greenhouse.

They spent the next two or three hours working in companionable silence, neither of them feeling the need for a steady stream of conversation. If one did talk, the other listened and offered a comment from time to time, but the pace and the atmosphere was decidedly relaxed.

By the time the last plant had been placed to John's satisfaction, the sun was beginning to sink below the tops of the trees. Leslie filled two glasses from the pitcher of lemonade that Nellie had left for them on the table near the pool. "Come have a drink, Dad. We've done enough for one day," she told him. She sank down in one of the cushioned chairs and leaned back with a sigh. Her body was protesting the cramped position of being on her knees for so long, but it was done with a feeling of accomplishment. She observed the transformation of the pool and surrounding area, brought about by the riot of color that now dotted the landscape, not without a sense of pride.

After a refreshing drink of the cool mixture, she eyed her father as he made his way toward her. "I think we've done a superb job, Mr. Garrison," she informed him in a pert tone.

He nodded his head. "I heartily agree, Miss Garrison. But then we've always worked well together." He reached for the glass of lemonade and drank thirstily. "Mmm, this just hits the spot." After seating himself, he looked questioningly at his daughter. "How about having dinner at the club this evening?"

"Sounds great," she promptly answered, giving him a lazy smile. "Is this Nellie's night out with the girls?"

"Yes, thank goodness."

"Do I detect a note of desperation in your voice?" she teased.

"That and more. I swear, Leslie, she's steadily getting worse. It's like being smothered in cotton," he said resignedly.

"I know, Dad. But she means well. At least I don't worry about your eating properly," she replied in a soothing voice. The battle between her dad and Nellie Temes had been going on for years. "By the way, how's business?"

This provided the perfect decoy, and for the next few minutes she listened as he told her about several new projects on the drawing board. As he spoke, Leslie found herself once again surprised by his youthfulness. He'd kept his body trim, and at age fifty-two he was quite a handsome man.

She was suddenly stricken with the remarkable notion that John and Cord would like each other. For in spite of her dad's mistake with Monica, the two men possessed a number of the same qualities—mainly stubbornness and determination.

Later, as she dressed for dinner, Leslie found her thoughts straying more and more to Cord. She remembered the moments, only a few hours ago, she'd spent in his arms. She was also aware that it was those moments that accounted for the added sparkle in her eyes. She'd caught her dad watching her several times during the day and she was certain he was more than a little curious. But her relationship with Cord was such a tenuous one it made discussing it an impossibility. Besides, her confidence in the outcome of that relationship was shaky at best.

She dressed for dinner with a strange premonition. It was impossible to put her finger on the reason for the feeling of dread that assailed her, but nevertheless it was there. She stared at herself in the mirror, seeing the burnished sleekness of her auburn hair, the calmness of her face, and the slender lines of her body, enhanced by the soft material of the blue dress she wore. It was uncanny how one could train one's facial muscles. Over the past three years she'd forced herself to present such a calm, cool facade to those closest to her, it was now done without thinking. Only one person knew her for the passionate woman she really was.

When Leslie and John entered the lounge of the Mariner's Club, several friends were already there and insisted that the Garrisons join them for a drink. It was a pleasant interlude, although at times Leslie felt like a teen-ager as she listened to the talk going on around her. She caught her dad's eye and smiled when one older lady in the group referred to the time

Leslie and her niece had been caught smoking in the pool house.

Later at their table John smiled and shook his head. "There's nothing more embarrassing than having one's childhood pranks paraded around for everyone to see."

Leslie laughed. "I agree. But at the time it was funny. Poor Mrs. Thorpe frightened us so by catching us, we both became ill. I think it was more from fright than from the tobacco."

Talk centered around generalities. Neither of them were ready to discuss what was really bothering them. They each knew the other had problems, but it went against their rules of long standing to pry.

Muted conversation and the tinkle of silver against china as they ate added to the feeling of contentment that slowly stole over Leslie. Her delicious and superbly prepared dinner merely added the finishing touches to a lovely evening. It gave her cause to question her earlier pangs of foreboding.

The white-coated waiter removed their plates and John had ordered coffee for them, when a peripheral movement to her right caused Leslie to look that way. Her muttered "Oh, no" caused her dad to quickly look toward the source of her annoyance.

"What the hell is he doing here?" he ground out in an undertone, as his gaze pinned his former son-in-law in his determined progress toward their table.

"I haven't the slightest idea, but from the direction he's taking, we'll soon know," she remarked drily.

The tall blond-headed man in question approached their table without the slightest show of embarrassment. The only sign of unease was in the tight set of his jaw, and this was discernible only to someone who knew him well. He was impeccably dressed, as usual, his dark jacket and light trousers fitting him to perfection.

He looked from John to Leslie and smiled. "What a coincidence," he spoke casually. "May I join you?" he asked while pulling out a chair and seating himself.

John threw him such a venomous look that even Leslie was shocked. He turned to his daughter. "Do you want him to join us?" he asked, ignoring Charles's attempt at friendliness.

"Er—yes." She spoke quickly. She knew her dad well enough to know that he'd have no qualms about removing Charles. And Charles would derive tremendous satisfaction from causing such a stir.

John pushed back his chair and stood. "I'll leave the two of you alone. I'm sure you must have some memorable moments to recall." With that he picked up his coffee and joined friends at a table across the room.

Leslie was tempted to throw the contents of her cup into Charles's grinning face, but some inner strength kept her from betraying her true feelings. She took a sip instead, exercising remarkable calm. "What brings you to Ft. Lauderdale, Charles?" she asked. Now that she knew him for what he really was, she was shocked that she'd once believed herself in love with him. He was like a chameleon, adapting to his surroundings without breaking his stride.

The lines of dissipation etched so firmly in his once handsome face left her with a feeling of sadness—a sense of waste. For a fleeting moment she felt pity for the man sitting across from her.

"A combination of business and pleasure," he replied off-handedly. "I took a chance that you might be visiting your dad. If I hadn't found you here, I'd planned on stopping by his place tomorrow."

Leslie gave him a look full of question, her eyes round with disbelief. "What on earth for?" she asked bluntly. *My God,* she thought wildly, *was it possible that Siri had been correct when she'd warned her that he was interested in a reconciliation?*

Charles refrained from answering immediately. Instead, he signaled the waiter. When the young man came over to the table, he ordered a Scotch and water and then leaned back in his chair. His gaze slowly worked its way from Leslie's face down her torso, visible above the table. "You've grown more beautiful, Les," he told her in a voice that left her chilled.

She'd heard that same petulant undertone many times before when he'd been denied something he especially wanted. Leslie's fists clenched in frustration. Damn him! He knew he had her at a disadvantage. Her father wasn't some doddering old man, but one perfectly capable of protecting his daughter. *But,* she silently vowed, *this is my fight, not Dad's.* She tipped her head forward slightly in acknowledgment of the compliment. "Thank you, Charles."

Her cool acceptance of his presence seemed to irritate him. A surge of anger could be seen in his blue eyes as he tried once again to shake her composure. "There's something different about you, some inner glow that I've never seen before. What's the reason behind it?"

The look she gave in return was distant and chilly. "I really don't know what you're talking about, Charles. And even if I did, I hardly think you'd be the one I'd choose to discuss my personal life with. Our marriage and subsequent divorce is not exactly conducive to lasting friendship," she replied crisply.

The dull flush that spread over his face and into the edge of his blond hair was clear indication that she'd scored a direct hit. He leaned forward, his anger out in the open now. "Why you little b—"

"Don't, Charles," she warned. "This is a private club and I'd hate to see you embarrassed by being thrown out. I think it would be a good idea if you finished your drink and left. I can't think of a single thing we have to say to each other."

He sat back heavily. The glass holding his Scotch and water was raised to his mouth and its contents drained in one swallow. There were several tense seconds before he spoke. "I'm sorry, Les. I shouldn't have lashed out like that." He gave her the old familiar smile of repentance that used to be his strongest target against her. "Am I forgiven?"

Seeing him deliberately go through the same routine that he'd used so many times before was equal to witnessing someone publicly humiliate themselves. Now it left her cold, emphasizing his completely selfish nature. "Of course," she heard herself saying, "no harm done."

Mistaking her easy capitulation for something else, he leaned forward and covered her hand that was toying with the stem of the water goblet. "Will you have lunch with me tomorrow? I know we've had our problems, but we're both adults. There's no reason why we can't enjoy each other's company occasionally. We've both had time to get over any little hurt we might have caused each other." He smiled expansively. "I'm thinking of taking an apartment here, Les. It could be like old times."

Slowly and deliberately she withdrew her hand, schooling her features to control the revulsion she felt at his pompous suggestion. "Exactly what are you getting at, Charles?" she bluntly asked.

"Come on, honey, don't play coy with me. I know from Siri that there's no one else in your life. And in spite of our problems, we did have some good times together." He gave her a look that spoke volumes, his gaze resting on the creamy skin exposed by the revealing neckline of her dress.

"Charles," she spoke softly, striving for control, "there can never be any sort of relationship between us." She had answered him as if speaking to a child. "We had our chance and we failed miserably."

His face underwent a dramatic change. Gone was the confidence of only moments ago, replaced by a look of defeat. He stared at her for a moment and then said, "What you're really saying is that I failed, isn't it?"

*Oh, yes,* she wanted to cry out, *you excelled in your ability to destroy any feelings I once had for you.* "Does it really matter who was at fault? It's over and, as you said, we both survived."

The angry outburst she expected didn't happen. Instead, Charles, for once since she'd known him, seemed to mature before her very eyes. He gave her a bitter smile, tinged with regret. "You landed with both feet on the ground, didn't you, Les? I suppose that's what I resent most. You continued your life as though I'd never existed. It's as though I passed through your life without causing a ripple."

"Oh, no, Charles. I assure you, your passing wasn't at all calm," she quickly disagreed. "But even if that were true, why should it bother you? Would it make you feel better if I appeared to be pining away, eagerly awaiting some gesture from you that you're ready to settle down?" She gave a short, mirthless laugh. "I'm sorry, Charles, but I find this entire conversation pointless."

"Will you let me take you home?" he asked quietly, his gaze never faltering under her suspicious one. "No tricks, Les, I promise. I'd simply like to take you home." He shrugged. "Call it what you will—I had to see you again."

Leslie glanced over to where her dad was sitting. He looked to be enjoying himself. She knew his reaction to Charles's taking her home would be one of displeasure, and yet she felt an inexplicable urge to do this one last thing. "All right, but let me tell Dad."

John listened to her plans with disapproval plainly written on his face, but he refrained from voicing such, for which Leslie was grateful. For even she was unable to understand clearly what prompted her to accept Charles's offer to take her home. Perhaps it was sympathy for a kindred soul—regret for what might have been. And even though she knew Charles for the unscrupulous person he was, at this particular moment she could afford to be generous. For it had taken considerable courage for him to come to see her.

During the drive Leslie was surprised at how easy it was to make conversation. Something Cord had once told her came to mind. He'd made the ridiculous statement that although she was legally divorced from Charles, emotionally she was still tied to him. At the time she'd reacted angrily. But now it suddenly dawned on her just how true his words were. She knew this last time with Charles was the one thing needed to erase him from her mind. She was over the hurt. No longer did she see him as the dashing, handsome man she'd fallen in love with. Now she saw him for what he was—a man without purpose, whose style of living had ceased to be satis-factory.

"What are your plans now, Charles?" she asked as they neared the street where her dad lived.

He shot her a wry grin. "Something that will shock you, I'm sure. My dad wants me to take over the Belgium office. I've held off giving him an answer until I saw you."

"And now?"

"Now I think I'll take it." He gave a curious glance at the dark colored car parked rather close to the entrance of the driveway, but dismissed it without another thought. "I need a change, and I think this is it."

"It sounds challenging. I hope it's what you're looking for, Charles."

After bringing the car to a stop, he switched off the engine and turned so that he was facing her. For several seconds he simply stared at her. "I'm sorry, Les. I really am." At her attempt to speak he said, "No, let me finish. I've been told by enough people, and finally realized myself, what a heel I was." He shook his head. "I know it's crazy, but for some reason I wanted you to know that I've changed."

"I'm glad to hear it," she replied softly. It was an awkward moment, but she was sincere in her wishes. The only drawback was the man himself. For his sake she hoped he meant it. She reached out and squeezed his hand that was laying on the console between the seats. "Good-bye, Charles, and good luck," she murmured and then turned to open the door.

Charles leaned over and placed one hand over hers on the door handle. He was quite close, and Leslie viewed his unexpected move apprehensively. He smiled at the uneasy look she gave him. "Don't worry, I'm not about to become difficult." One hand caught her chin as his lips touched hers in a gentle kiss. He drew back, regret mirrored in his face. "Good-bye, Les."

She stepped from the car with a mixture of sadness and relief. She moved back onto the grassy verge and watched as he slowly backed the car down the driveway and then turned and headed back the way they'd come.

At that moment, she noticed the other car parked at the driveway's entrance and wondered whose it was. Ignoring it, she gave in to the relief that swept over her, equating the feeling to being cleansed by a bright spring shower. She hugged her arms about her body and lifted her face to the moon, visible through the spreading limbs of the large oak tree.

Suddenly her life took on a different meaning. She was ready for the future—a future with Cord, however he wanted it.

She walked around the house to the patio entrance and unlocked the sliding doors. When she entered, MacGregor went through his ritual welcome. Leslie sat down on the sofa and ruffled the coat of the aging terrier, rubbing his ears and scratching his head.

Even the dog seemed to sense the excitement that emanated from his young mistress.

## CHAPTER TEN

Leslie had just let MacGregor out for his nightly run when the insistent ringing of the doorbell broke through the silence of the house. She glanced at her watch as she hurried through to answer, surprised to see that it was close to midnight.

Nellie had forgotten her key again, Leslie thought as she reached for the knob and opened the door. "You're lucky . . ." The words died on her lips. For not Nellie but Cord was leaning against the wall. One arm was stretched across the opening, the other held in readiness to push the small black button again.

Leslie stared at him, unable to speak. All the air from her lungs seemed to rush to her head, causing her to cling to the edge of the door to keep from falling. "H-how did you know where to . . . to find me?" she finally got out.

"I spoke with Miriam," came the cold reply. He pushed his body away from the wall and stepped inside, pulling the door from her grasp and closing it. Leslie didn't move for several seconds. Things were moving too fast, and certainly not in the manner in which she'd planned.

First Charles, and now Cord. She searched his face for some sign of the lover who had held her in his arms less than twenty-four hours ago. But all she saw was suppressed fury in the unyielding lines of his features. "I want to talk with you, Leslie," he told her in a harsh voice, completely devoid of gentleness.

"Of course," she murmured huskily. She turned to lead the way to the den when her arm was gripped by fingers of steel. Cord swung her around. "Not here. Get your purse and a wrap," he ground out savagely.

"Please," she whispered, her other hand going to his hold on her arm. "You're hurting me." His grip slackened, but he didn't release her. He steered her toward the hallway, seemingly afraid to let her out of his sight.

Her mind was in a turmoil as she walked beside him. She wondered if her absence had provoked such an outrageous display of temper. "Did you have a nice trip?" she asked in a small voice and then immediately could have bitten her tongue. It sounded asinine and stupid. "I didn't look for you to be back so

171

soon, Cord. You should have let me know when to expect you."

"Obviously." He made a deprecatory gesture with one hand. "I'm not in the mood for small talk, Leslie," he informed her roughly. "Leave a note for your dad so he won't worry," he instructed.

"But surely we won't—"

The sentence was never finished. Cord reached for her, his strong arms crushing her to his chest. His mouth swooped down on hers in a brutal and savage kiss. Leslie tried to turn her head to one side, but he became incensed by her resistance and clamped one hand to the nape of her neck. His tongue forced her lips apart ruthlessly, and she felt the taste of blood as his teeth ground against her lips.

Suddenly the love she'd felt earlier for him burgeoned into pure rage at his rough treatment. This isn't love, her senses shrieked, this is a brutal assault! She twisted her body with all her might until she was free of the feel of his mouth on hers. Both her hands went unerringly to his chest and pushed against him. Cord momentarily slackened his hold, and in that split second Leslie's hand collided with the granite hardness of his cheek.

The print of her fingers showed red against the unusual pallor of his skin. "Get out!" she cried in a trembling voice, stumbling backward from the unleashed violence burning in his face and eyes. She brought her hands up and pressed them against her burning cheeks, dizzy from the emotion-filled scene.

Fear and anger waged an equal battle within her slender frame as she watched Cord struggle to control his wrath. It seemed an eternity passed as they stared at each other. The loosened collar of his shirt and the dark suit he wore attested to the fact that he'd worn a tie earlier. His thick, dark hair was not in its usual state of neatness. From all indications he'd run his fingers through it more than once. It softened the harshness of his features, Leslie mused illogically.

He stood with feet apart, his jacket pushed back and his thumbs hooked in the waistband of his trousers. Never in her life had Leslie been subjected to such a brutal and nerve-wracking examination as he was subjecting her to. The stupor she found herself in was broken when he began the slow, pantherlike tread toward her.

Leslie's gaze darted toward the sliding doors, her mind measuring the distance. If she could only reach the door in time, she'd be safe. Cord observed her nervous calculations with a sneer. "I don't think so, my dear," he laughed harshly, lengthening his stride to cover the distance between them in two steps. He stopped so close in front of her, the tips of her breasts brushed against his chest. She could feel the rapid thudding of his heart joined by the frantic pounding of her own. He made no effort to touch her. "Write the note, Leslie."

She stared at him, his expression unreadable. There was no softness, no hint of gentleness in his tone or manner. He must have read her uncertainty, for he said, "If I've frightened you, I'm glad. But just to set your mind at ease, I've yet to hit a woman. Although I have to admit, I've come closer this night than I ever thought possible." He then surprised her by stepping around her and moving over to stand at the large window.

Leslie walked over to the desk and found a small pad and a pen. She quickly wrote a short message for her dad, and then paused to look questioningly at Cord. "What time shall I say I'll be back?"

He turned and met her gaze, his mood only slightly less frosty than before. "Don't. If he has doubts about me, he can get in touch with George," was his curt reply.

Leslie sighed, but did as he said. She'd seen a side of him tonight that had frightened her. She'd witnessed him in various moods—teasing, demanding, loving. But nothing had prepared her for the deep, smoldering anger he'd shown.

After attaching the note to the telephone, she picked up her small bag and the light wrap she'd worn earlier. "I'm ready," she murmured, her voice sounding far braver than she was feeling. Cord merely flicked a stormy glance her way before he came over and grasped her elbow and ushered her out to the car.

It didn't take her long to realize that they were leaving Ft. Lauderdale and heading toward the east coast. She cast an apprehensive glance at his rigid profile, but could tell nothing from the indomitable thrust of his chin. A few more miles of stony silence was all she could endure. "May I ask where we're going?" a hint of her former stubbornness crept into her voice.

"There's a beach house not far from here that I'm interested in. This seems like an excellent time to really look it over," came his stiff reply.

Leslie's natural curiosity demanded more. "Are you going to buy it?"

"Perhaps." He shrugged his broad shoulders. "I'm not sure," which told her exactly nothing.

"Are you sure it will be all right for us to see the place this late?"

For the first time since he'd arrived that evening there was a softening of his features. His lips curved in a brief smile. "I have the key, so you can stop worrying. We're not likely to be taken for trespassers."

She sat back, somewhat relieved. Skulking around some deserted beach house at midnight was not exactly her ideal pastime.

"Tell me, Leslie, what prompted you to visit your father this weekend?" Cord asked, never taking his eyes off the road.

The question caught her unawares. She wondered what he would say if she confessed that the thought of waiting all weekend for him to call had been more than she could bear. She leaned her head back against the seat, her eyes on the darkened landscape

175

flashing by. "I was overdue for a visit. Dad's going through a bad stretch at the moment and I thought I might be able to help." This was partially true.

"And were you?"

"I hope so. He's already filed for divorce, so the worst is over." Cord didn't comment, and once again they lapsed into silence. Leslie turned her head so that she could watch him through her lashes. She longed to reach out and touch him and reassure herself that he was real and not a figment of her imagination.

Her love for him was slowly driving her crazy. One minute she was convinced he cared for her—the next found her agonizing over the fact that he was only amusing himself with her. Caring as she did left her defenseless.

Leslie was so deep in her thoughts, she was unaware when Cord left the main highway and turned on to a firmly packed dirt road that ran parallel with the ocean. She looked around her in surprise as they came to a stop.

The beam of the headlights bathed the timber and masonry structure straight ahead in their bright glow. From where she sat in the car Leslie could see a screened-in porch that ran the width of the house. It was nestled in a grove of palms and banana trees.

She turned to Cord, an excited smile on her face. "So far I like what I see. It reminds me of a place we used to go to when I was a little girl."

Cord removed the keys from the ignition and

opened the door. "Would you care for a guided tour?" he asked, evidently pleased by her enthusiasm.

"Indeed I would." She quickly opened her door and got out, meeting him in front of the car. Cord caught her elbow firmly and guided her over the uneven turf as they made their way toward the entrance. Leslie waited impatiently for him to select the right key and open the door.

The house was beautiful, but could hardly be described as a simple beach house. It consisted of a large kitchen, equipped with every conceivable gadget. There were also two bedrooms, a bath, and a den. During the inspection a small frown began to form on Leslie's smooth brow. The house bore none of the usual signs of having been closed for months. And what surprised her even more were the well-stocked cupboards as well as the amount of food in the refrigerator. "How long have the present owners had the house on the market?" she asked curiously, noting the sparkling condition of the kitchen.

Cord leaned against the butcher-block counter, his arms crossed over his chest, and watched her. "For several months I believe. Do you like it?"

She turned to face him. "I love it. Are you really considering it?"

He held up the keys, a smile tugging at the corners of his mouth. "I've already bought it."

Leslie gave him a wry grin. "You've been teasing me all along, haven't you?"

Suddenly the room seemed filled with electricity. She moved away from the refrigerator, uncertain as to what to do or say next. Cord was still watching her, his expression unreadable. Under his disturbing gaze she began to fidget.

After what seemed like an interminable wait, he pushed away from the counter and closed the space between them. Leslie viewed his approach with wariness. It required all her courage not to turn and run. Her gaze dropped to his chest. When his arms reached for her, she willingly allowed her body to slump against his.

Cord slipped one long finger beneath her chin and tilted her head back to meet his burning gaze. There were still lines of tension in his face that left her bewildered. "Don't you think it's about time you told me who your date for the evening was? I'm aware that neither of us swore an oath to be faithful, but last night was very special to me. And to you, or so I thought."

Leslie closed her eyes for a moment and rested her forehead against his comforting touch. Now the curtain was lifted; she could see the reason for his strange behavior. She gathered her courage together as she sought to explain. She raised her head and met his gaze squarely. "I did go out to dinner with Dad. We'd almost finished eating when Charles came over to our table." She licked her lips in a nervous gesture before going on. "When he asked to join us, I said yes." She could feel his hold on her tighten noticeably. "Cord, I only did it to avoid a scene. Both men were ready to go at each other like two snarling dogs."

"Go on," he commanded in an icy voice.

She sighed. "There's nothing much to tell. Charles had a drink and then he brought me home."

Cord transferred his hold to her arms and shook her. "I want to know every word that was spoken, every gesture, damn you," he exploded. "Call me a masochist or whatever suits you, I don't care. But I have to know what it is about that bastard that fascinates you so. When I saw him kiss you, it took every ounce of will power I possessed to keep from dragging him from that car and killing him. And if he ever touches you again, I will!"

Leslie stood transfixed, her mouth open like someone suddenly bereft of her senses, suddenly realizing that the car parked near her dad's driveway had been Cord's. Her next reaction was one of guilt, causing her to lash out defensively. "How dare you spy on me," she hurled at him. She twisted from his hold and stepped back. "Yes, he kissed me, but it didn't mean any more to me than last night did to you," she cried in a trembling voice.

The combination of hurt, guilt, and frustration made her careless in her choice of words. But Cord's disruptive influence in her life had left her with nerves as taut as a bowstring. The fact that she was fully cognizant of his reputation with women—and her own love for him—was slowly eating away at her. "As you just pointed out, we didn't vow to be faithful to each other, and, quite frankly, I doubt you could be faithful to one woman if you tried."

She turned on her heel and rushed from the room, bent on reaching the front door. She reached her goal easily enough and grasped the handle. When the door failed to open, she naturally assumed it was stuck and added force to her efforts.

"As appealing as you are in that position, I think I should point out that the door is locked." Leslie spun around to encounter Cord's sardonic gaze and his nonchalant stance in the doorway leading from the kitchen.

Her fists were clenched in frustration as she fought back the urge to stamp her feet. Lifting her head proudly, she said, "Will you please unlock the door?"

"No," came his blunt reply. He reinforced his refusal by folding his arms across his chest, giving the impression of one prepared to wait indefinitely. "We haven't finished talking," he informed her with deadly calm.

Leslie was the first to look away. She left her position by the door and walked over and stared out the window at the moonlight shining on the white sandy beach. Tears pricked the surface of her eyes, blurring her vision. The relief and happiness she'd experienced after leaving Charles had somehow been lost in the midst of flaring tempers and the misunderstanding that had sprung up. Her meeting with Cord had gone wrong from the beginning. Instead of the tender reunion she'd imagined, they were snarling at each other, lashing out with reckless disregard for each other's feelings.

The touch of his hand on her waist caused her to jump slightly. She looked over her shoulder at him, the heartache she was suffering mirrored in her lovely face.

"Leslie, let's stop this tearing each other apart," he said hoarsely, taking her by the arm and leading her over to the sofa. He gently pushed her down and then followed. The close proximity did nothing to calm her frazzled state.

Cord turned so that he was facing her and slid one arm along the back of her head, his fingers lightly resting on her shoulders. "Look at me," he softly demanded. When she did as he asked, he said, "Tell me why Charles kissed you."

*If you muff this,* the little voice inside her cautioned, *you'll never get another chance.* Leslie took a deep breath and squared her shoulders. "It's not at all what you think. At first he seemed to be much the same as when we parted. He even suggested that we start seeing each other again. But after I convinced him that there was nothing left for us"—she shrugged—"he calmed down and revealed a side of his personality I'd never seen."

"And did this revelation appeal to you?" he snapped.

"Not in the way you mean. I was pleased that he

was beginning to show some sign of maturity. But other than that, I felt nothing. As for the kiss, it was a very chaste one. There was no passionate farewell involved," she stated simply.

Cord was silent for several moments, his gaze through half-closed lids never leaving her face. Leslie withstood his harsh scrutiny with an outward calm that was deceiving.

"Do you plan to offer encouragement at various intervals in this rehabilitation that you seem so certain is taking place?"

She shook her head. "No. He's going to Belgium to take over the management of the firm's branch there. I sincerely doubt I'll ever see him again," she replied. Her body was slowly relaxing as Cord's face began to lose its strain. She suddenly felt an urgent need to touch him.

Without giving herself time to think, she placed one hand on his muscled thigh, a look of love showing in her eyes that only a blind man could fail to see. "Charles is not the one I'm in love with, Cord. And whether you believe me or not, I'm quite sick of talking about him," she said spontaneously.

The fingers that had been barely touching her shoulders, now eased down and caressed her creamy throat. There was firm but gentle pressure as he drew her to him. His other arm reached out and pulled her close. He rested his face against the silky softness of her hair. "I'm sorry, honey. I know I behaved like a monster. But when I saw him kiss you, I went beserk," he murmured. He tilted her head back, dropping soft feathery kisses on her face, her neck, and on down to the shadowy cleft between her breasts.

Leslie endured his lovemaking passively until the smoldering coals of desire ignited into a burning flame. When the slight trembling started in her slender frame, Cord's mouth covered hers in a deep, hard kiss. There was none of the savage punishment of before, but neither was it soft and gentle. He accurately sensed her need for reassurance and carried her through the tide of passion that engulfed her.

He lifted his head so that he could see her face, his eyes glowing with triumph at the drugged expression on her face. "I hope your father isn't expecting you back tonight, because I have no intention of taking you home." He came to his feet and then reached down and swung her up in his arms.

Leslie was only half aware of him speaking. Her body and mind were both too attuned to the feel of Cord's touch to notice or care about anything else. It was only when he came to a halt beside the bed and gently set her on her feet that some semblance of reality took over. The light brush of his fingers against her skin as he dealt with the fastening of her dress evoked the first sign of resistance. "Cord . . ."

"Sssh," he whispered, slipping the dress from her body with one deft move. She heard the catch of his breath as the moonlight coming in through the window bathed her in its glow. He bent his head and kissed the throbbing fullness of her breasts, his hands cupping them tenderly. His tongue teased the sensitive, erect peaks, and Leslie once again felt the now familiar stirrings in her veins that only his hand, his lovemaking could assuage.

She slid her arms around his neck and arched her body against the firm hardness of his thighs, refusing the tiny spark of regret to surface. With Cord she was resigned to live for the moment, even if those moments were to be her only memories.

In seconds his clothes joined hers in a heap on the floor. When he lifted her and placed her on the bed, Leslie could see that he too was just as wrought up in the moment as she was. In that split second she hugged that fact to her, finding immense satisfaction in the knowledge that she could arouse him to such a state. Her pleasure in that small victory was soon lost when Cord's hand began moving over her body, discovering again the secret places of arousal.

She lifted one hand and grasped the back of his head to still the teasing of his lips on her face and neck. Instinctively his lips met hers with a smothered groan. Their bodies softly moved against each other, reveling in the contact of skin against skin. Her doubts forgotten, Leslie was burning from the heat he had so easily ignited in her. His loving hands were never still, touching, stroking, transferring her body from all earthly cares.

This time Leslie didn't have to be prodded into taking part in the beauty of their lovemaking. She knew now that instead of being only the receiver of passion, it was just as important that she share this moment of ecstasy with Cord.

Only the moonlight was witness to their intermingled cries of pleasure as their hands and mouths became totally committed to the oneness of subjecting each other to the delights and exquisite pleasures of their love.

For Leslie there was a brief moment of awareness —when it became impossible not to compare this unbelievable happening with her unhappy relationship with Charles. She knew Cord's body in a way she'd never desired to know Charles's. All the warmth of her affectionate nature was now channeled toward creating the same heart-stopping pleasure for Cord as he gave her.

Untutored as she was in the ways of making love, it wasn't long before Leslie's hands were incapable of anything other than clutching Cord's broad shoulders as wave upon wave of desire shot through her body. Cord was the master and she the pupil. She caught and held him close, a smothered gasp of excitement slipping from between her parted lips as she attuned herself to the slow, almost languorous pace Cord set to their lovemaking. Each touch, each passion-filled kiss was matched with equal fervor by Leslie, and at the final moment Leslie felt as if her very soul had been set on fire, combining with Cord's in an explosion that catapulted them skyward, their descent, slow and gentle.

Later, the silvery room was silent except for their gentle breathing. "This has got to stop," Cord murmured against the firm softness of her breasts, his breath warm against her skin.

Leslie's fingers that were threaded in his thick hair became still. She slowly withdrew her hand, bracing herself for what was about to come.

Reading her withdrawal with uncanny accuracy, he raised his head, his sharp gaze missing nothing. "I've a fairly good idea what's going on in that pretty little head of yours, so before you start making mountains out of molehills, let me explain." He shifted his position so that the upper part of his body was supported by his elbows. His large hands framed her face as one thumb gently caressed the corners of her lips. "I'm not to content to snatch a few hours with you." He grinned. "My appetite, where you are concerned, is never satisfied."

"Are you suggesting that we live together?" she asked as calmly as she could manage.

Cord's gentle laughter sounded in her ear. "Yes, my little pessimist, that's exactly what I'm suggesting. I've had my fill of watching you deal with aging millionaires and rich playboys with roving eyes. I want my ring on your finger so there'll be no mistake who you belong to."

Leslie didn't respond for a moment, wondering if she'd heard correctly. Cord's hands slid to her shoulders and gripped her tightly. "Are you deliberately trying to provoke me, Leslie?" His rugged breathing fanned her cheeks.

"No, Cord," she answered quite honestly.

"Well then?" he demanded huskily, his body tense. She couldn't control the impish grin that appeared on her face. And yet she was also vitally aware that this huge, sensitive man was baring his soul, exposing a vulnerability she doubted he'd ever shown in his life.

She lifted her arms to encircle his neck and raised her lips to his. "Yes," she whispered just before his mouth covered hers. It was a gentle kiss, full of meaning. Cord raised his head to look at her. "I hope you can plan a wedding in three days, because I refuse to wait a minute longer."

"Three days?" she exclaimed. "I can't possibly be ready by then," she protested and then cried out laughingly as he buried his face between her neck and shoulder and bit her in mock anger.

"Stop it!" she squealed and when still not happy with her response Cord began to inflict other forms of equally pleasurable punishment. By then Leslie was limp from laughing. "All right, all right," she weakly agreed. "But I'll probably be the only bride to appear in rags," she pointed out.

Cord rolled over on his back and gathered her close. "I don't gave a damn if you arrive in a barrel, honey. My patience is at an end." He pressed her head against his chest. "Do you want to stay here or at my place in Coral Gables until then?" he asked her. "Later on we can decide on a place to live permanently."

"Does it really matter?" she returned, her fingers playing with the dark hair on his chest. "As long as we're together, I can be happy anywhere." She looked thoughtful for a moment. "There's also the small matter of my job."

He turned so that he was facing her. "Do you want to continue working?"

Leslie watched him closely as she asked her own question. "Would you mind if I did?"

He smiled and leaned down and kissed her forehead. "Not at all, if it's what you want."

She heaved a small sigh of relief. "I'll resign immediately," she answered.

Cord frowned, unable to understand her reasoning. He rested his chin on one hand and smiled. "Explain, please."

"Well," Leslie laughed, "if you'd refused and made sounds like a domineering male, I'd have resented it. As you were so nice about it, I'd *rather* spend all my time with you."

"I love you, Leslie Garrison. You've yet to disappoint me," he murmured.

His words were like a soothing balm. She'd doubted him for so long, and now her fears were allayed. "You finally said it," she whispered, a suspicious glimmer appearing in her eyes.

Cord smiled. "You haven't exactly been a loudmouth on the subject yourself." He shrugged. "But your actions gave you away. It was simply a matter of waiting for you to recognize and accept the inevitable." He slid one hand down over her satin-smooth skin to rest possessively on the curve of her hip. "I almost felt sorry for you at times, but from the moment I first saw you, I knew you were the one for me."

Leslie lifted a hand to smooth his cheek, the shimmer in her eyes now grown to tears. "I love you," she whispered.

No words were spoken for quite a while in the room; there was no need for them. The two lovers were unaware of anything but their need for each other and the new found joy of their love. The incoming tide was the only sound, and the only witness, the fabled man in the moon.